Dance Class

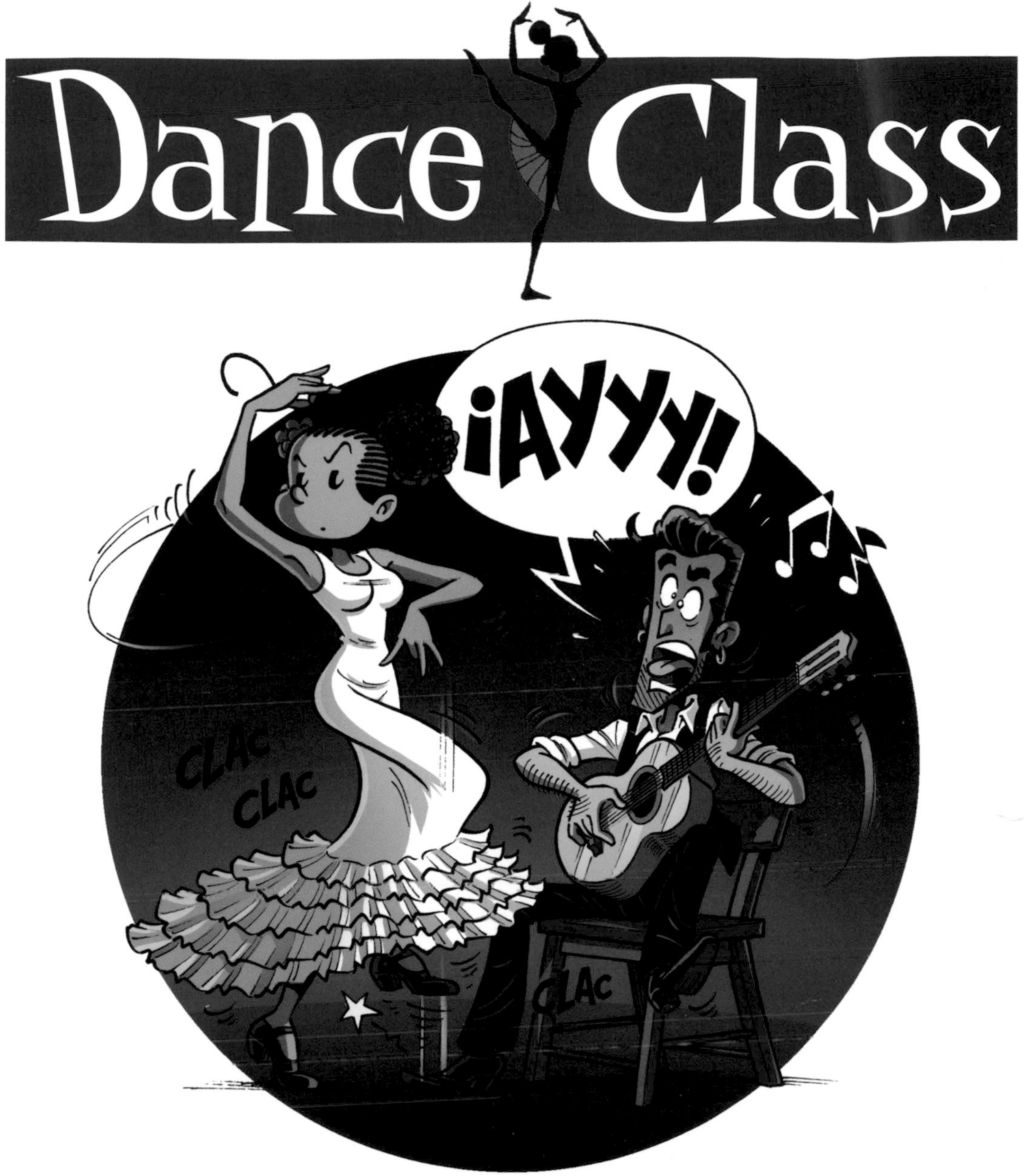
¡AYYY!
CLAC
CLAC
CLAC

Béka • Writer
Crip • Artist
Maëla Cosson • Colorist

PAPERCUTZ
New York

Dance Class Graphic Novels available from PAPERCUTZ™

Béka and Crip
Dance Class
So, You Think You Can Hip-Hop?
PAPERCUTZ

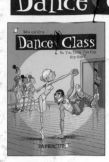

#1 "So, You Think You Can Hip-Hop?"

Béka and Crip
Dance Class
Romeos and Juliet
PAPERCUTZ

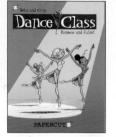

#2 "Romeos and Juliet"

Béka and Crip
Dance Class
African Folk Dance Fever
PAPERCUTZ

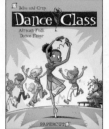

#3 "African Folk Dance Fever"

Dance Class

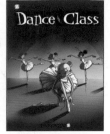

#4 "A Funny Thing Happened on the Way to Paris..."

Béka and Crip
Dance Class
To Russia, With Love
PAPERCUTZ

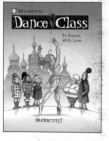

#5 "To Russia, With Love"

Béka and Crip
Dance Class
A Merry Olde Christmas
PAPERCUTZ

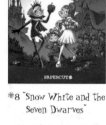

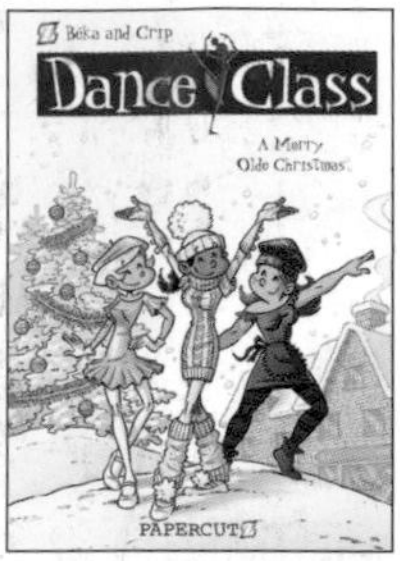

#6 "A Merry Olde Christmas"

Béka and Crip
Dance Class
PAPERCUTZ

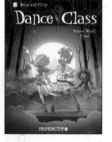

#7 "School Night Fever"

Béka and Crip
Dance Class
Snow White and the Seven Dwarves
PAPERCUTZ

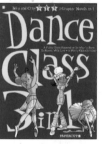

#8 "Snow White and the Seven Dwarves"

Béka and Crip
Dance Class
Dancing in the Rain
PAPERCUTZ

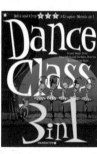

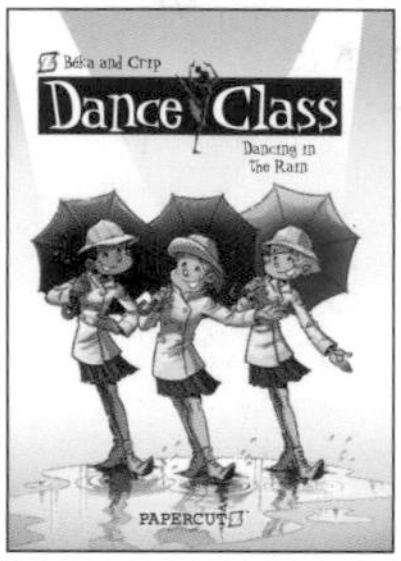

#9 "Dancing in the Rain"

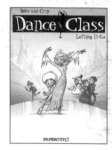

Béka and Crip
Dance Class
Letting It Go
PAPERCUTZ

#10 "Letting It Go"

Béka and Crip
Dance Class
Dance with Me
PAPERCUTZ

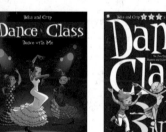

#11 "Dance with Me"

Dance Class
3 in 1
PAPERCUTZ

DANCE CLASS 3 IN 1 #1

Dance Class
3 in 1
PAPERCUTZ

DANCE CLASS 3 IN 1 #2

Dance Class
3 in 1
PAPERCUTZ

DANCE CLASS 3 IN 1 #3
COMING SOON!

SEE MORE AT PAPERCUTZ.COM

Also available digitally wherever e-books are sold.

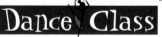

Dance Class

DANCE CLASS #11
"Dance with Me"
BÉKA — Writer
CRIP — Artist
MAËLA COSSON — Colorist
MARK McNABB — Production
JOE JOHNSON — Translation
WILSON RAMOS JR. — Lettering
JEFF WHITMAN — Editor
JIM SALICRUP
Editor-in-Chief

Special thanks to
CATHERINE LOISELET

ISBN: 978-1-5458-0632-6

Printed in China
January 2021

Papercutz books may be purchased for business or promotional use. For information on bulk purchases please contact Macmillan Corporate and Premium Sales Department at (800) 221-7945 x5442.

Distributed by Macmillan
First Papercutz Printing

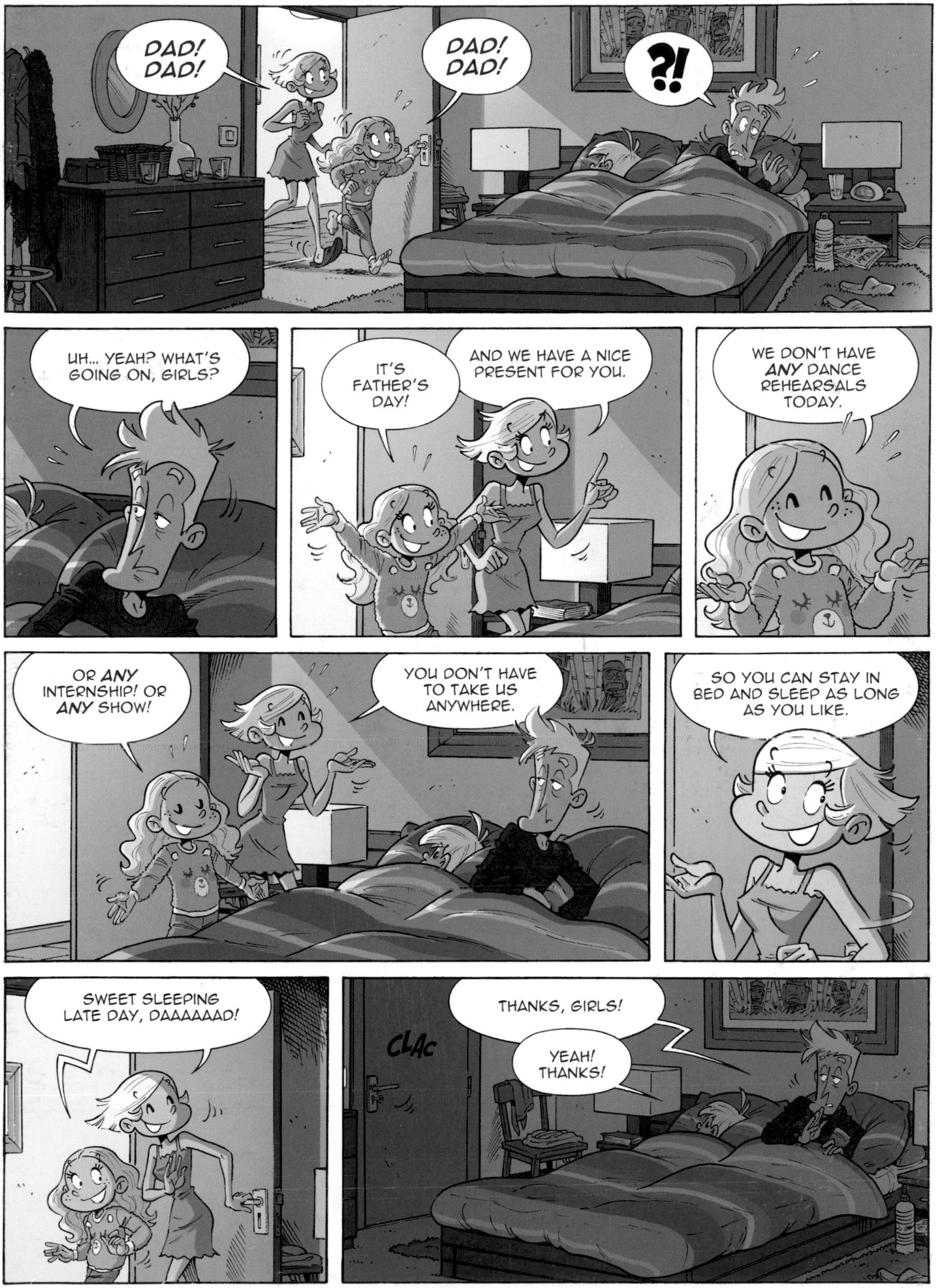
DAD! DAD!
DAD! DAD!
?!
UH... YEAH? WHAT'S GOING ON, GIRLS?
IT'S FATHER'S DAY!
AND WE HAVE A NICE PRESENT FOR YOU.
WE DON'T HAVE ANY DANCE REHEARSALS TODAY.
OR ANY INTERNSHIP! OR ANY SHOW!
YOU DON'T HAVE TO TAKE US ANYWHERE.
SO YOU CAN STAY IN BED AND SLEEP AS LONG AS YOU LIKE.
SWEET SLEEPING LATE DAY, DAAAAAAD!
CLAC
THANKS, GIRLS!
YEAH! THANKS!

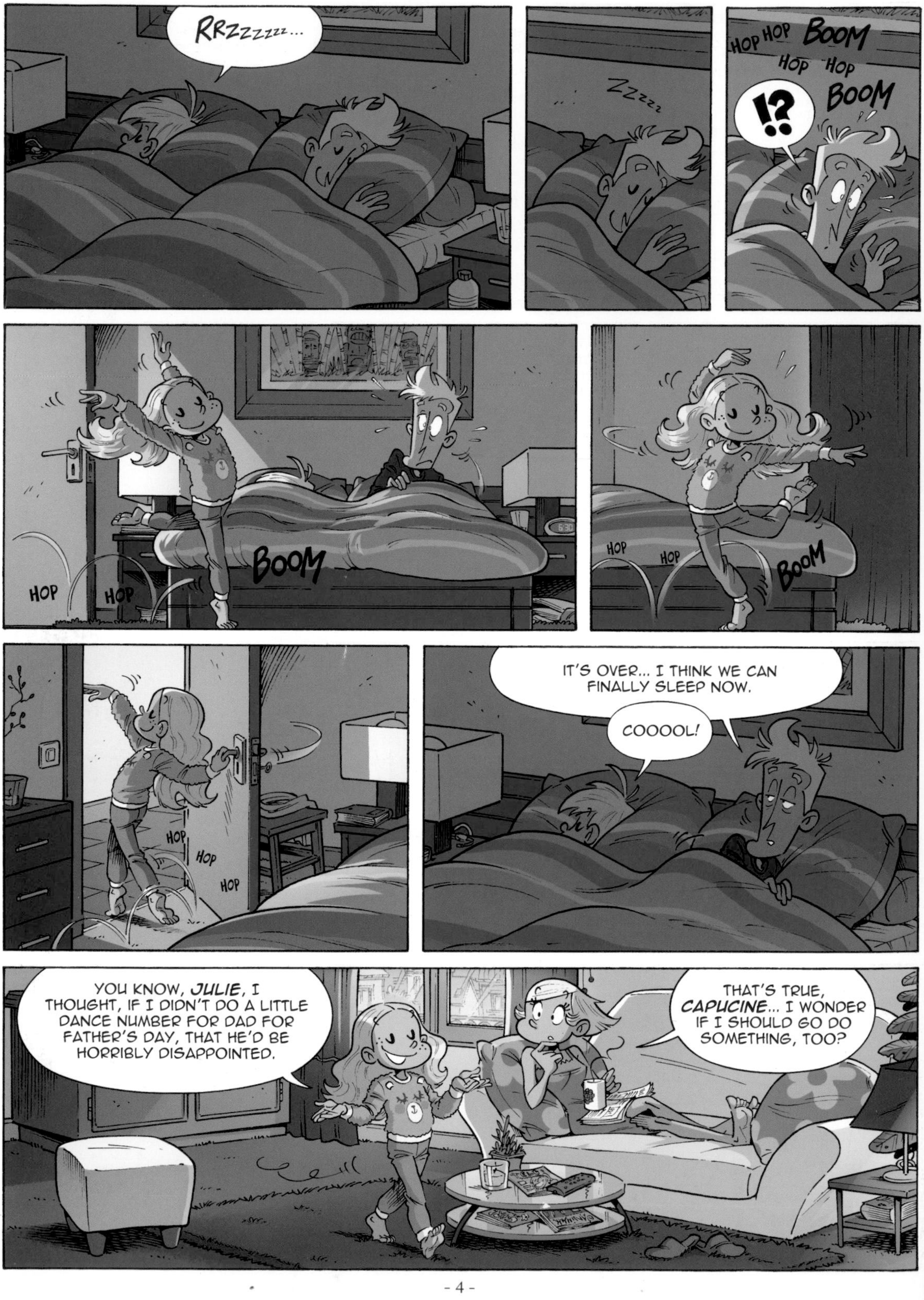
RRZzzzzz...
Zzzzz
HOP HOP BOOM
HOP HOP
BOOM
!?
BOOM
HOP
HOP
HOP
HOP
BOOM
HOP
HOP
HOP
IT'S OVER... I THINK WE CAN FINALLY SLEEP NOW.
COOOOL!
YOU KNOW, JULIE, I THOUGHT, IF I DIDN'T DO A LITTLE DANCE NUMBER FOR DAD FOR FATHER'S DAY, THAT HE'D BE HORRIBLY DISAPPOINTED.
THAT'S TRUE, CAPUCINE... I WONDER IF I SHOULD GO DO SOMETHING, TOO?

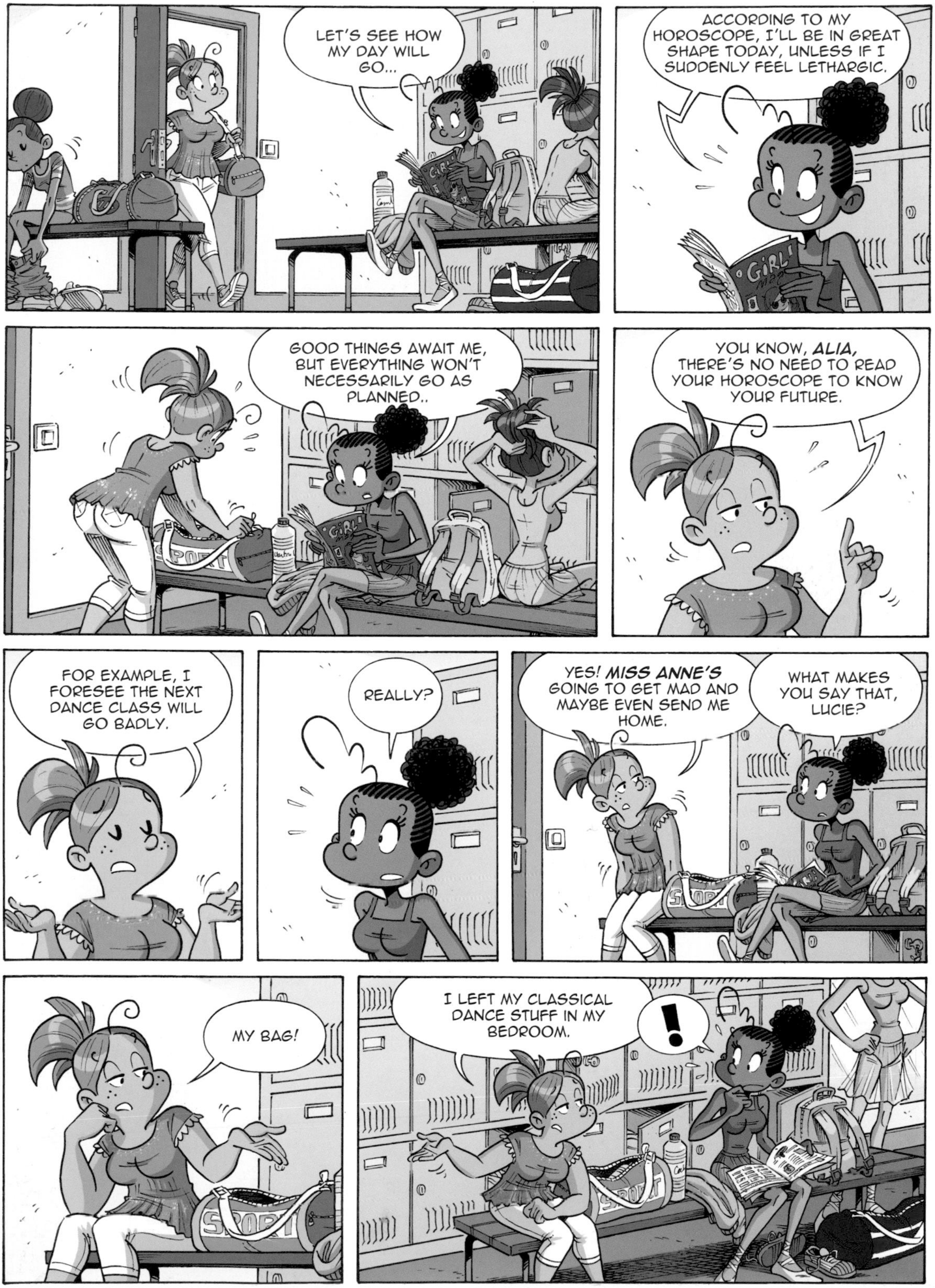
LET'S SEE HOW MY DAY WILL GO...
ACCORDING TO MY HOROSCOPE, I'LL BE IN GREAT SHAPE TODAY, UNLESS IF I SUDDENLY FEEL LETHARGIC.
GOOD THINGS AWAIT ME, BUT EVERYTHING WON'T NECESSARILY GO AS PLANNED..
YOU KNOW, ALIA, THERE'S NO NEED TO READ YOUR HOROSCOPE TO KNOW YOUR FUTURE.
FOR EXAMPLE, I FORESEE THE NEXT DANCE CLASS WILL GO BADLY.
REALLY?
YES! MISS ANNE'S GOING TO GET MAD AND MAYBE EVEN SEND ME HOME.
WHAT MAKES YOU SAY THAT, LUCIE?
MY BAG!
I LEFT MY CLASSICAL DANCE STUFF IN MY BEDROOM.
!

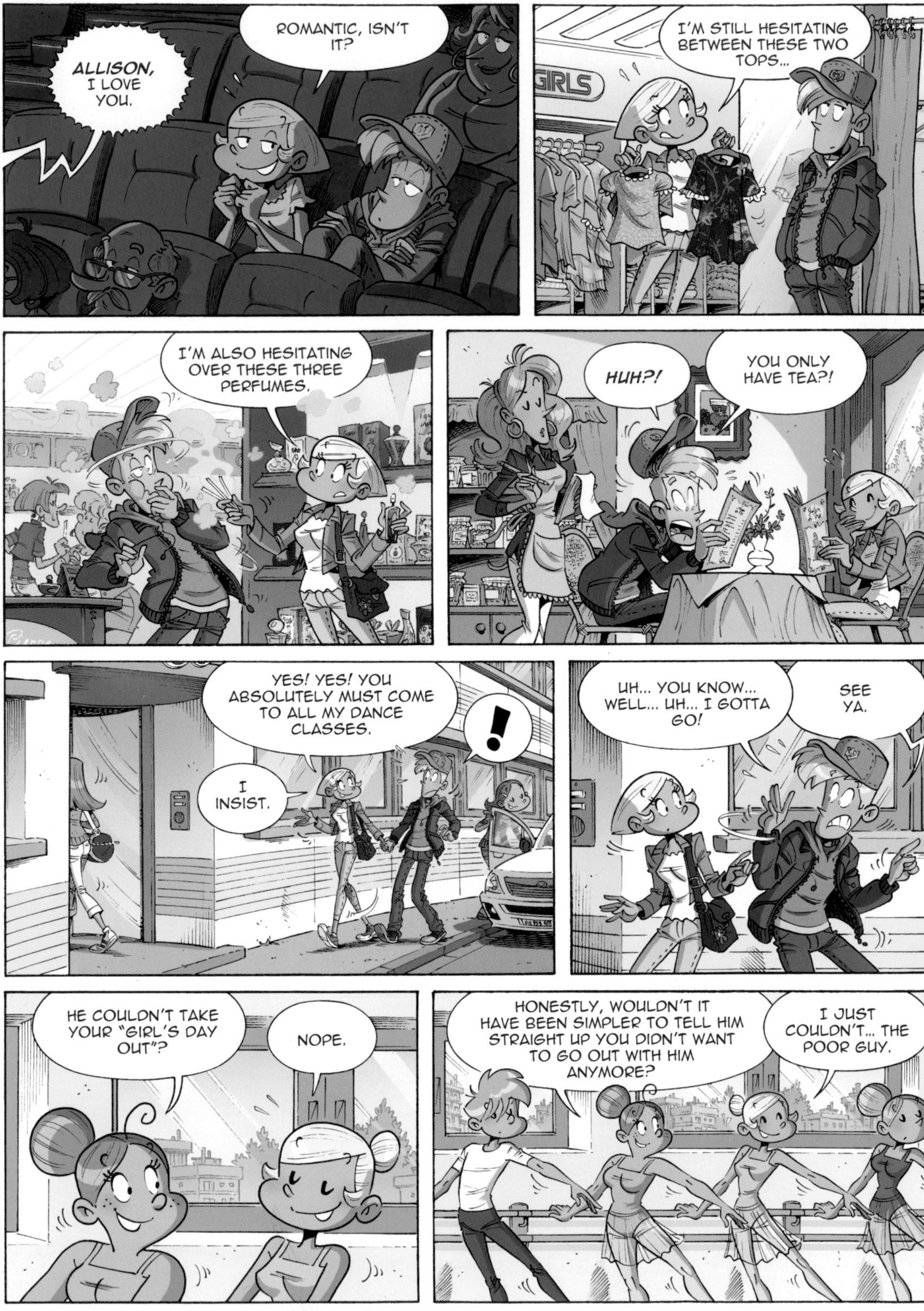
ALLISON, I LOVE YOU.
ROMANTIC, ISN'T IT?
I'M STILL HESITATING BETWEEN THESE TWO TOPS...
GIRLS
I'M ALSO HESITATING OVER THESE THREE PERFUMES.
HUH?!
YOU ONLY HAVE TEA?!
YES! YES! YOU ABSOLUTELY MUST COME TO ALL MY DANCE CLASSES.
!
I INSIST.
UH... YOU KNOW... WELL... UH... I GOTTA GO!
SEE YA.
HE COULDN'T TAKE YOUR "GIRL'S DAY OUT"?
NOPE.
HONESTLY, WOULDN'T IT HAVE BEEN SIMPLER TO TELL HIM STRAIGHT UP YOU DIDN'T WANT TO GO OUT WITH HIM ANYMORE?
I JUST COULDN'T... THE POOR GUY.

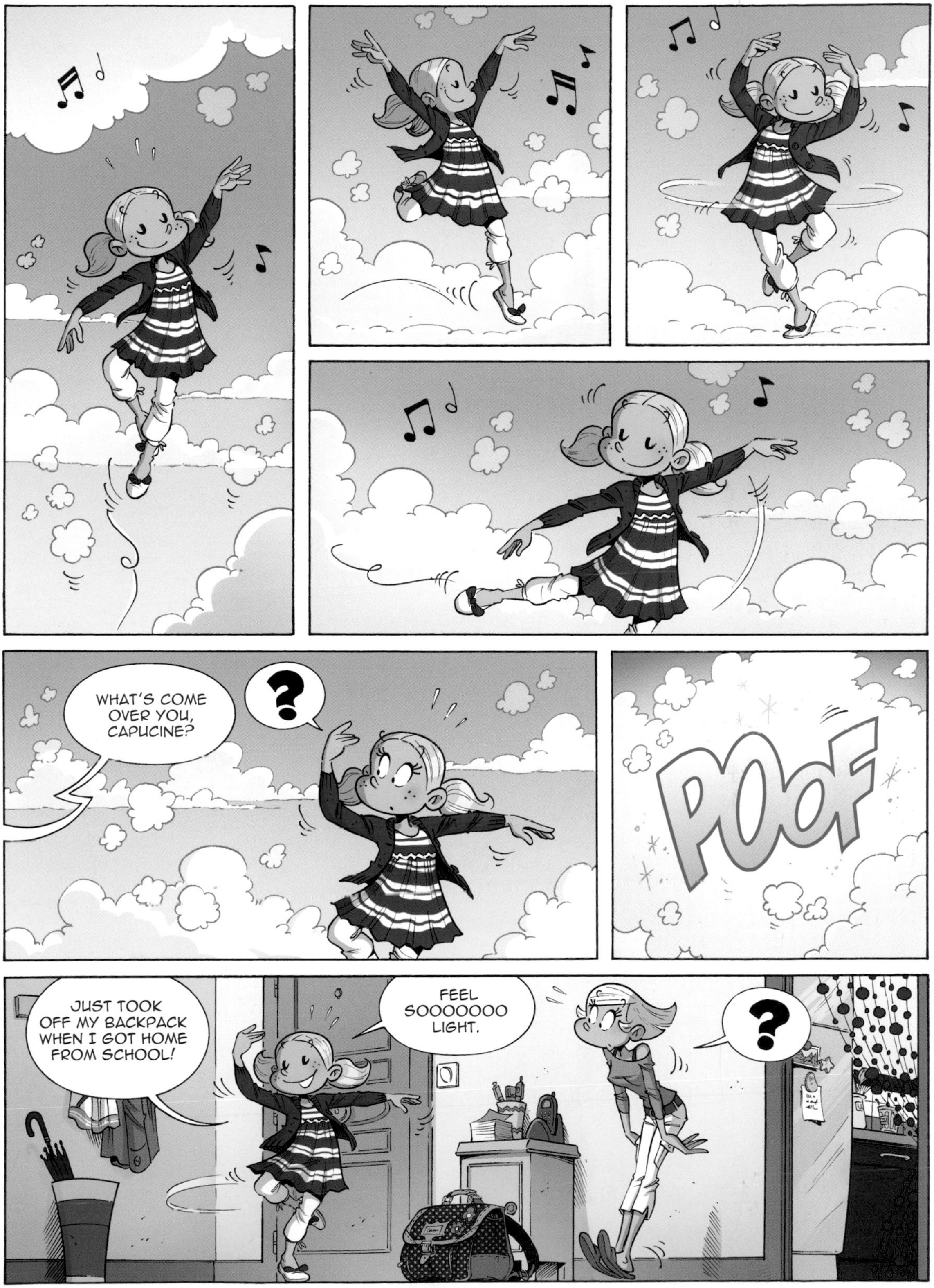
WHAT'S COME OVER YOU, CAPUCINE?
?
POOF
JUST TOOK OFF MY BACKPACK WHEN I GOT HOME FROM SCHOOL!
FEEL SOOOOOOO LIGHT.
?

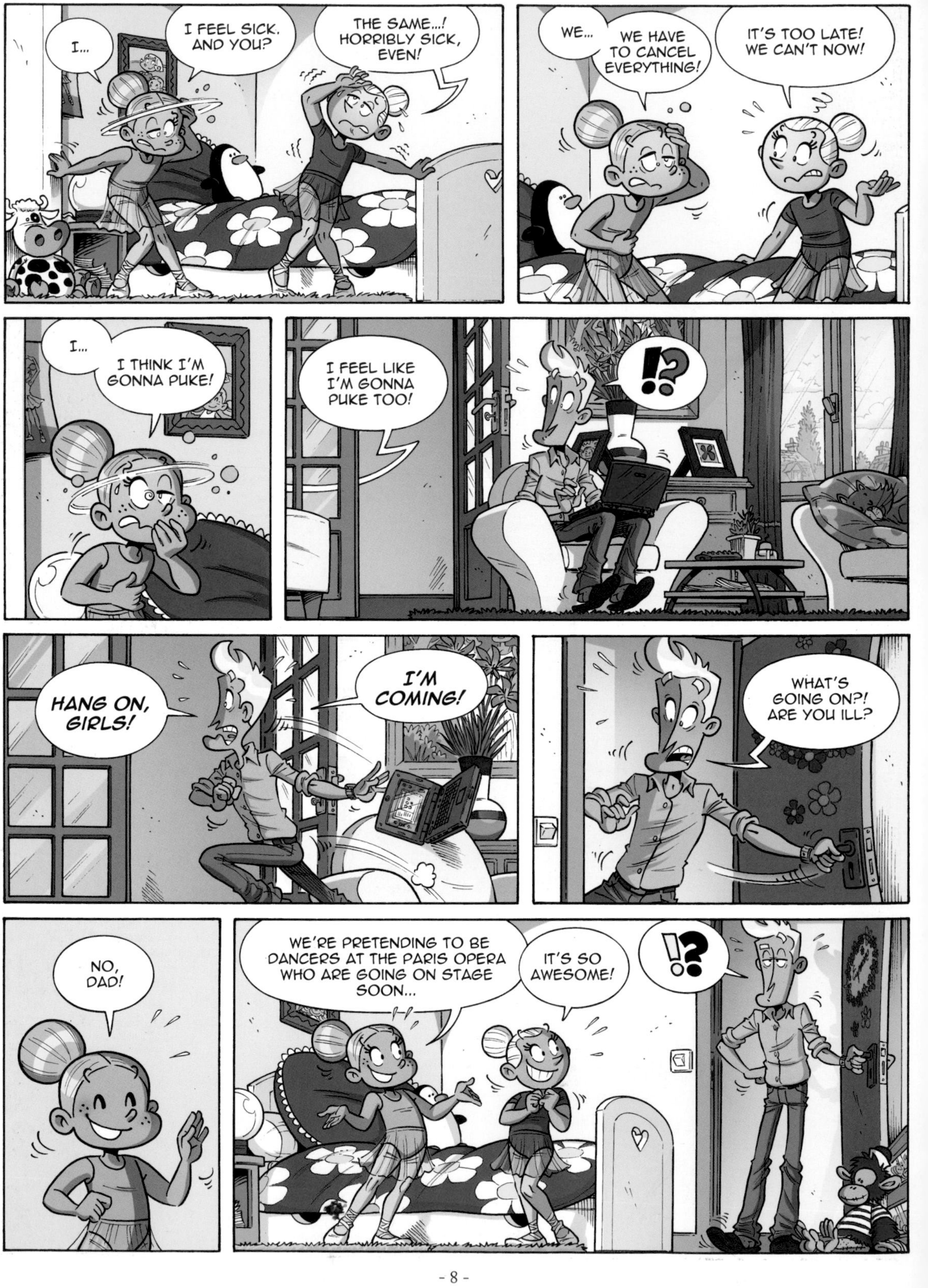
I...
I FEEL SICK. AND YOU?
THE SAME...! HORRIBLY SICK, EVEN!
WE...
WE HAVE TO CANCEL EVERYTHING!
IT'S TOO LATE! WE CAN'T NOW!
I...
I THINK I'M GONNA PUKE!
I FEEL LIKE I'M GONNA PUKE TOO!
!?
HANG ON, GIRLS!
I'M COMING!
WHAT'S GOING ON?! ARE YOU ILL?
NO, DAD!
WE'RE PRETENDING TO BE DANCERS AT THE PARIS OPERA WHO ARE GOING ON STAGE SOON...
IT'S SO AWESOME!
!?

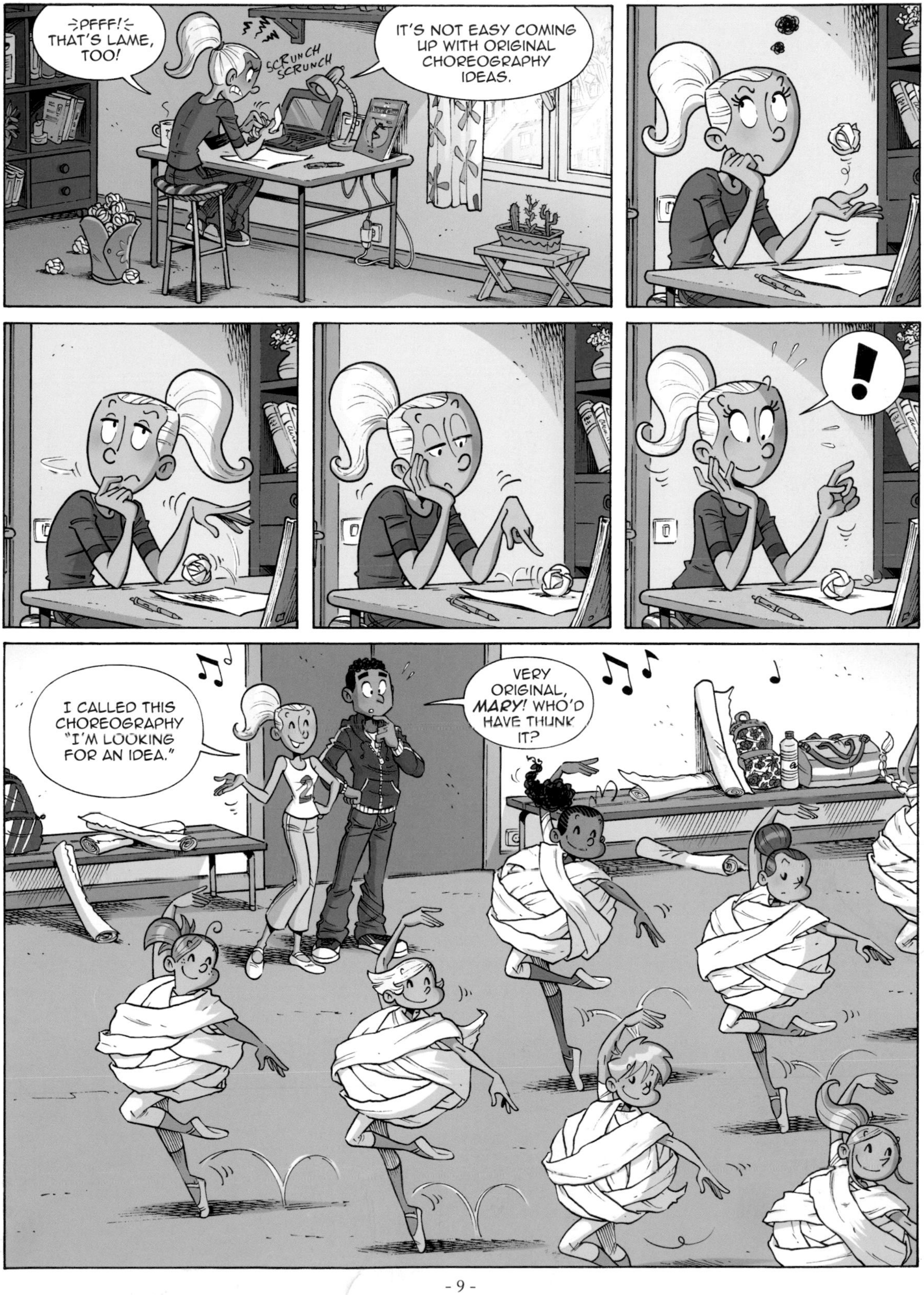

PFFF! THAT'S LAME, TOO!
SCRUNCH SCRUNCH
IT'S NOT EASY COMING UP WITH ORIGINAL CHOREOGRAPHY IDEAS.
!
I CALLED THIS CHOREOGRAPHY "I'M LOOKING FOR AN IDEA."
VERY ORIGINAL, MARY! WHO'D HAVE THUNK IT?

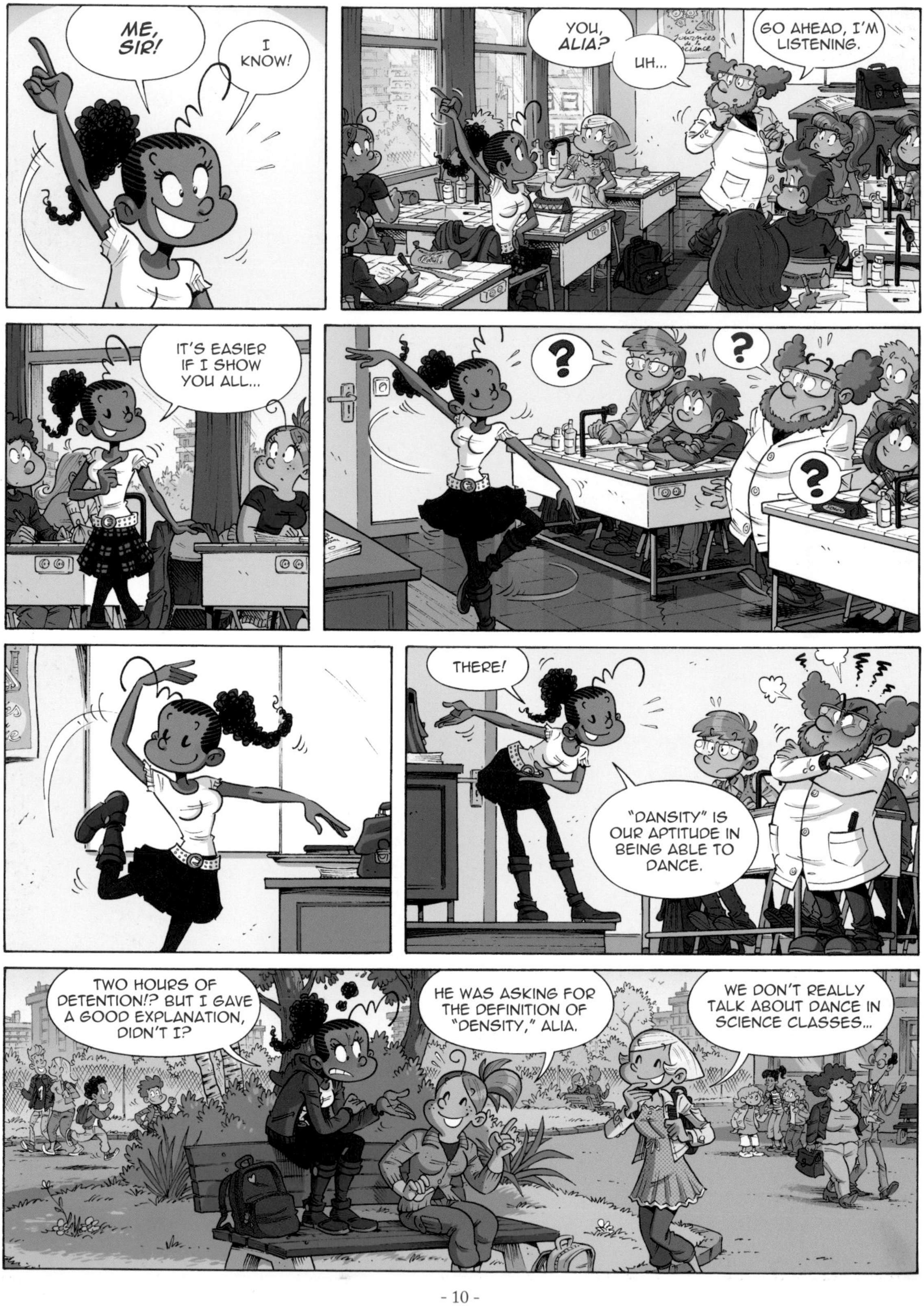

ME, SIR!
I KNOW!
YOU, ALIA?
UH...
GO AHEAD, I'M LISTENING.
IT'S EASIER IF I SHOW YOU ALL...
?
?
?
THERE!
"DANSITY" IS OUR APTITUDE IN BEING ABLE TO DANCE.
TWO HOURS OF DETENTION!? BUT I GAVE A GOOD EXPLANATION, DIDN'T I?
HE WAS ASKING FOR THE DEFINITION OF "DENSITY," ALIA.
WE DON'T REALLY TALK ABOUT DANCE IN SCIENCE CLASSES...

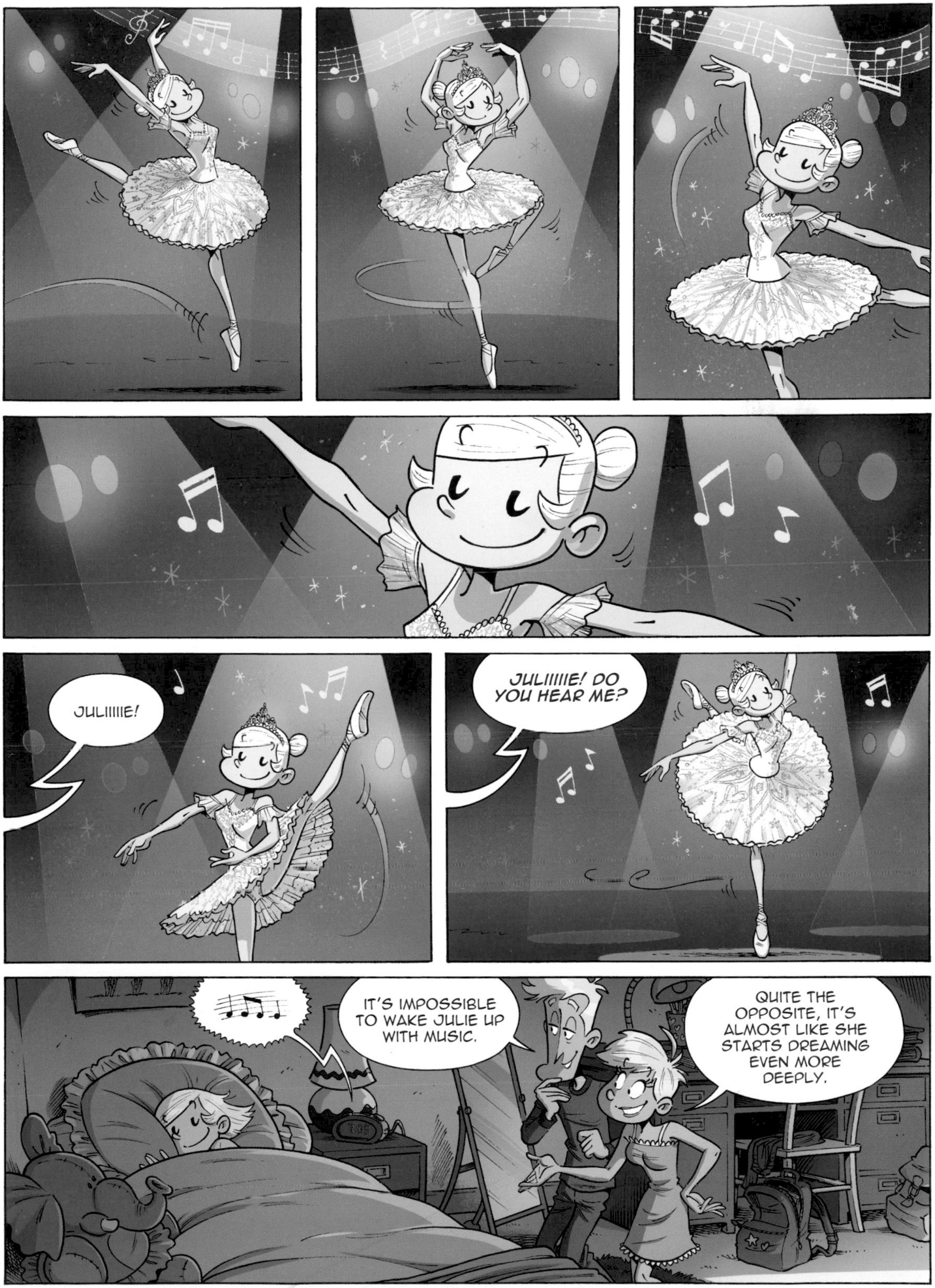
JULIIIIIE!
JULIIIIIE! DO YOU HEAR ME?
IT'S IMPOSSIBLE TO WAKE JULIE UP WITH MUSIC.
QUITE THE OPPOSITE, IT'S ALMOST LIKE SHE STARTS DREAMING EVEN MORE DEEPLY.

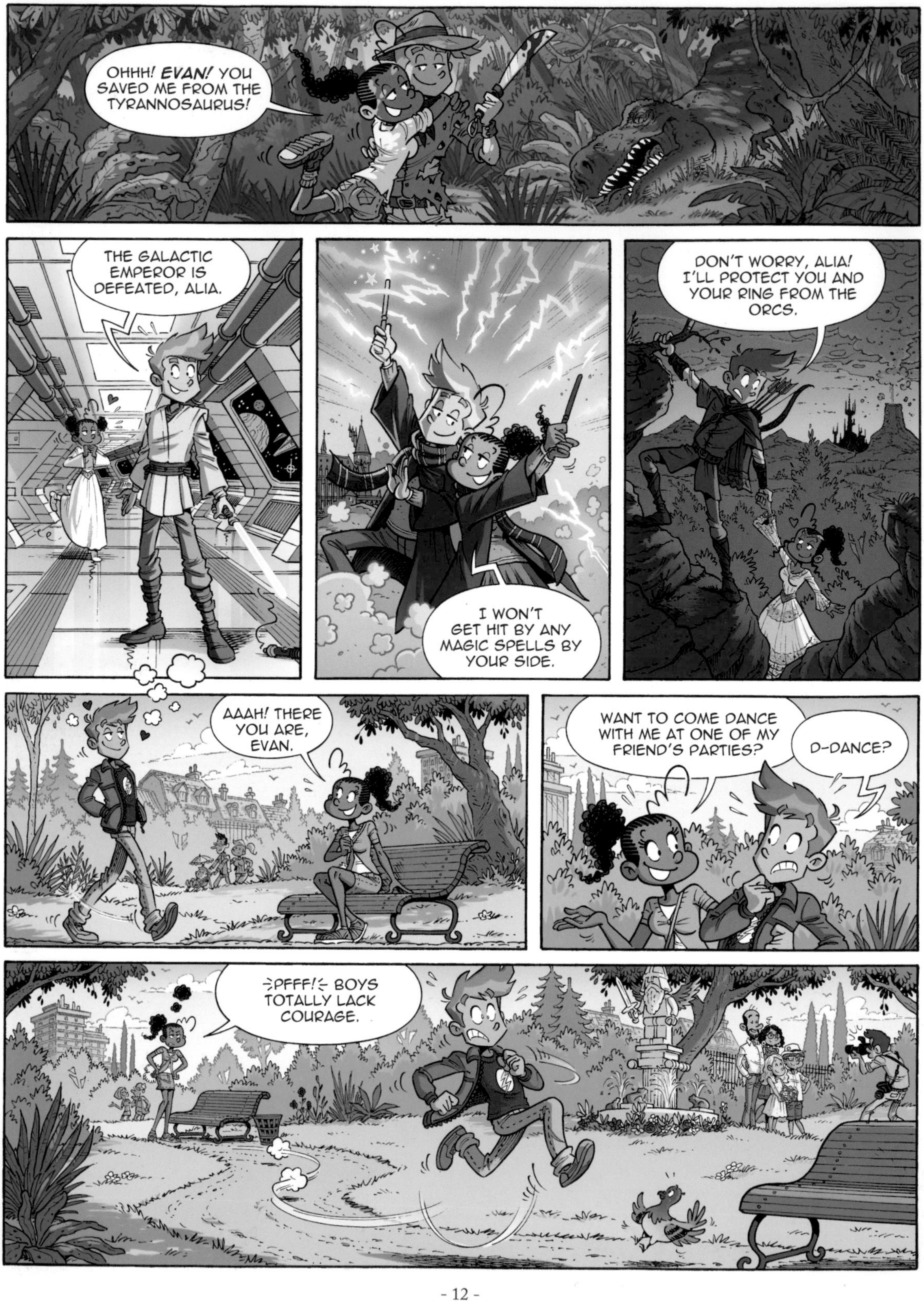
OHHH! EVAN! YOU SAVED ME FROM THE TYRANNOSAURUS!
THE GALACTIC EMPEROR IS DEFEATED, ALIA.
I WON'T GET HIT BY ANY MAGIC SPELLS BY YOUR SIDE.
DON'T WORRY, ALIA! I'LL PROTECT YOU AND YOUR RING FROM THE ORCS.
AAAH! THERE YOU ARE, EVAN.
WANT TO COME DANCE WITH ME AT ONE OF MY FRIEND'S PARTIES?
D-DANCE?
PFFF! BOYS TOTALLY LACK COURAGE.

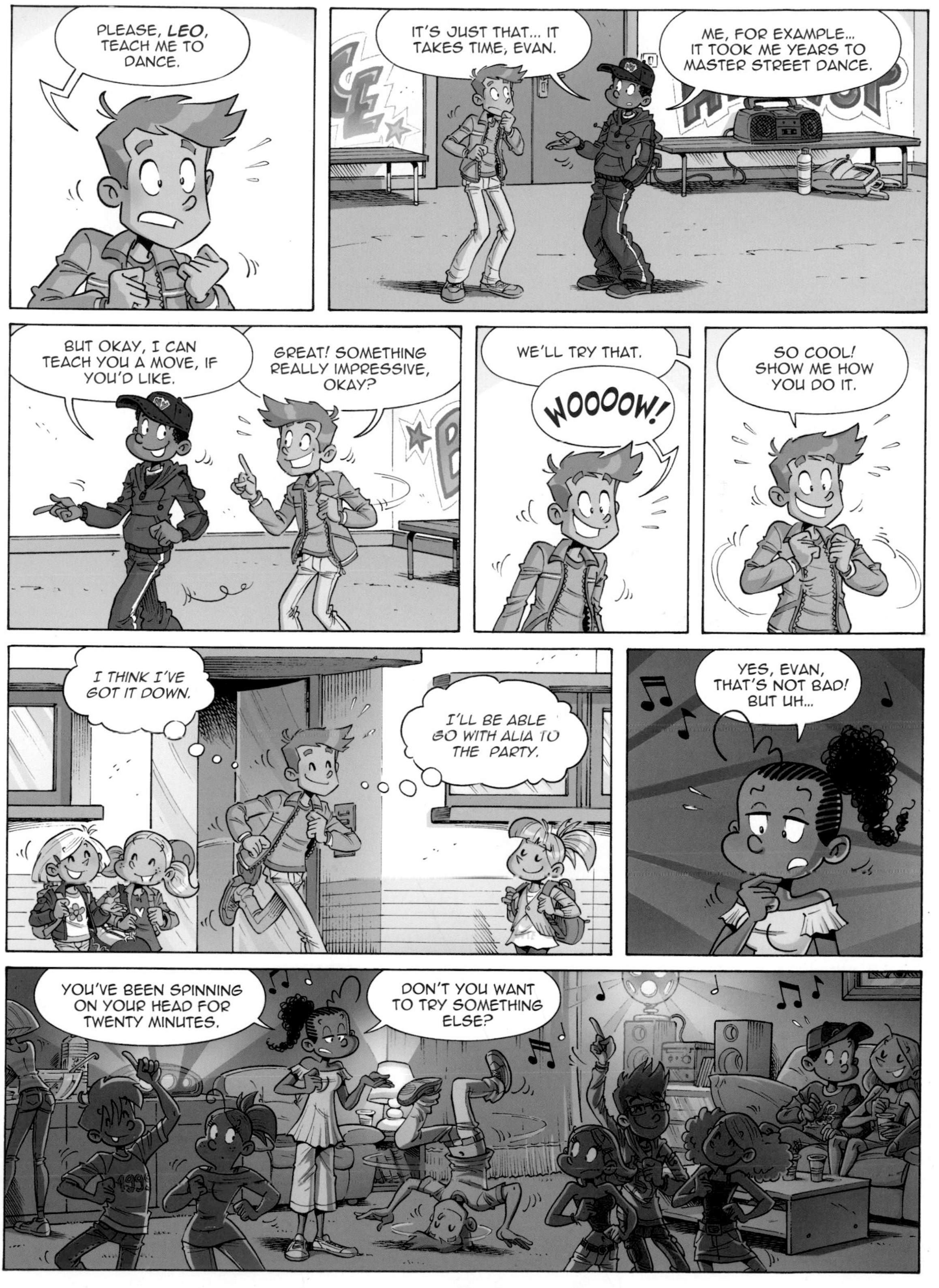
PLEASE, LEO, TEACH ME TO DANCE.
IT'S JUST THAT... IT TAKES TIME, EVAN.
ME, FOR EXAMPLE... IT TOOK ME YEARS TO MASTER STREET DANCE.
BUT OKAY, I CAN TEACH YOU A MOVE, IF YOU'D LIKE.
GREAT! SOMETHING REALLY IMPRESSIVE, OKAY?
WE'LL TRY THAT.
WOOOOW!
SO COOL! SHOW ME HOW YOU DO IT.
I THINK I'VE GOT IT DOWN.
I'LL BE ABLE GO WITH ALIA TO THE PARTY.
YES, EVAN, THAT'S NOT BAD! BUT UH...
YOU'VE BEEN SPINNING ON YOUR HEAD FOR TWENTY MINUTES.
DON'T YOU WANT TO TRY SOMETHING ELSE?

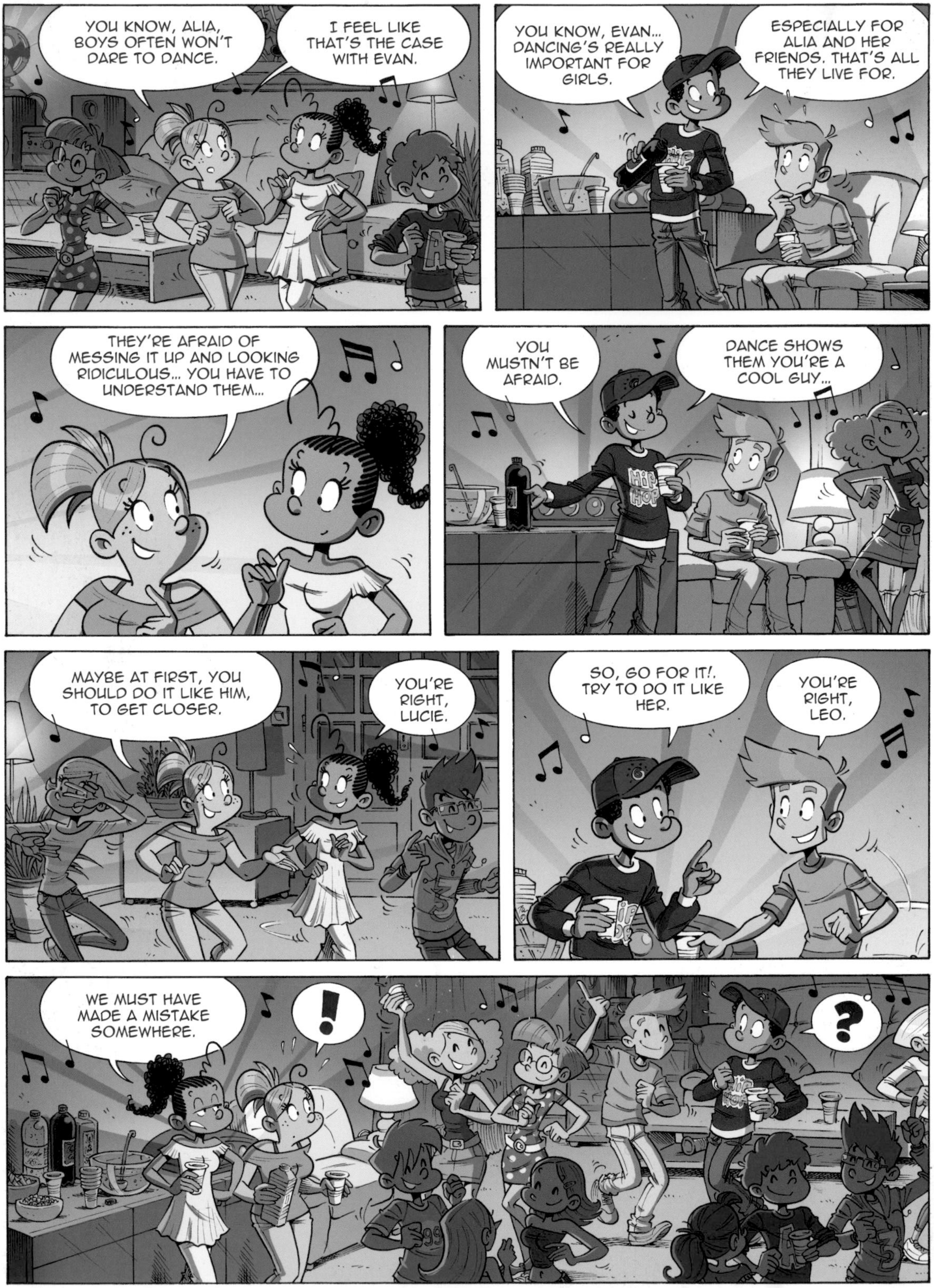

YOU KNOW, ALIA, BOYS OFTEN WON'T DARE TO DANCE.
I FEEL LIKE THAT'S THE CASE WITH EVAN.
YOU KNOW, EVAN... DANCING'S REALLY IMPORTANT FOR GIRLS.
ESPECIALLY FOR ALIA AND HER FRIENDS. THAT'S ALL THEY LIVE FOR.
THEY'RE AFRAID OF MESSING IT UP AND LOOKING RIDICULOUS... YOU HAVE TO UNDERSTAND THEM...
YOU MUSTN'T BE AFRAID.
DANCE SHOWS THEM YOU'RE A COOL GUY...
MAYBE AT FIRST, YOU SHOULD DO IT LIKE HIM, TO GET CLOSER.
YOU'RE RIGHT, LUCIE.
SO, GO FOR IT!. TRY TO DO IT LIKE HER.
YOU'RE RIGHT, LEO.
WE MUST HAVE MADE A MISTAKE SOMEWHERE.
!
?

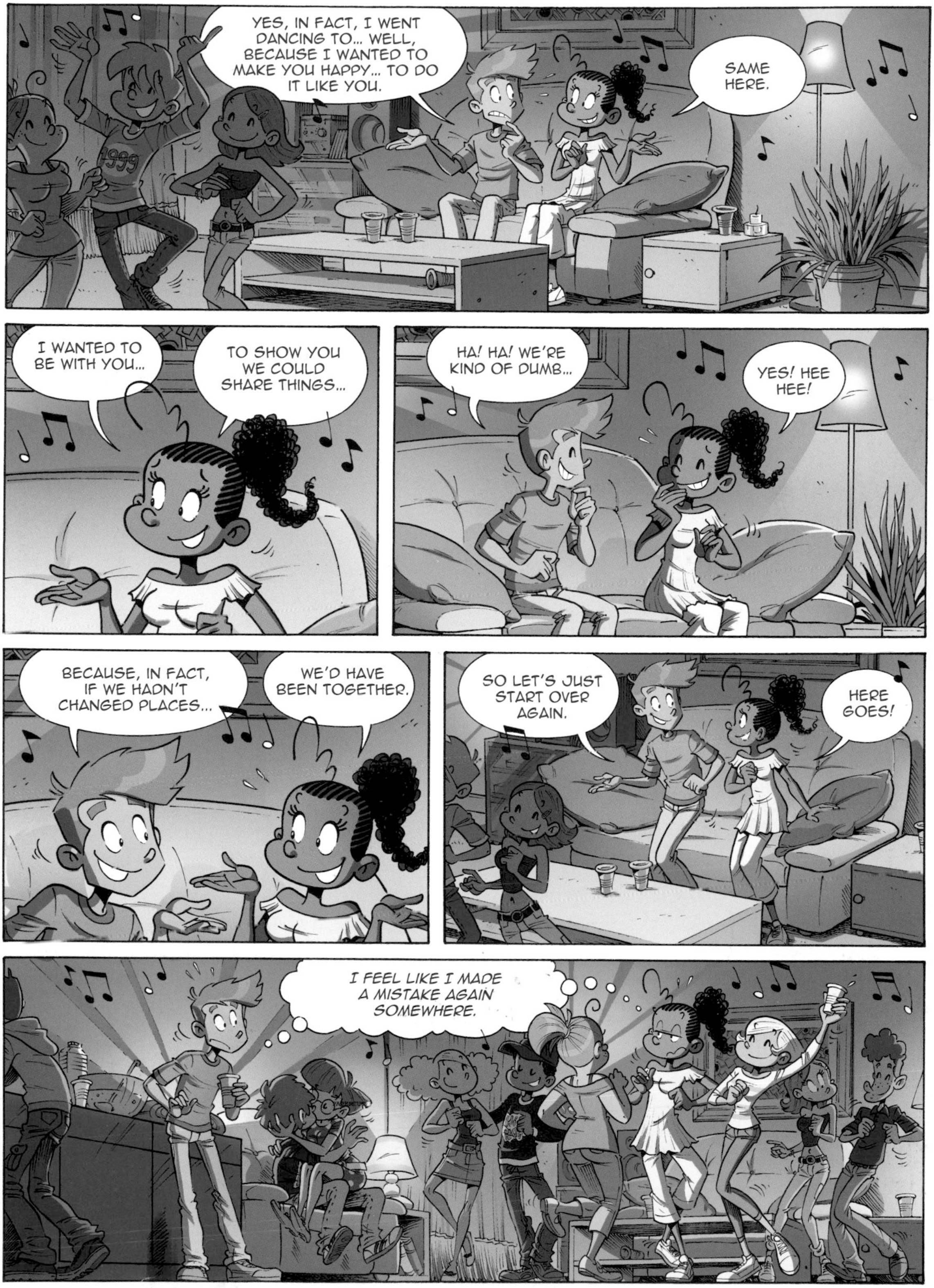
YES, IN FACT, I WENT DANCING TO... WELL, BECAUSE I WANTED TO MAKE YOU HAPPY... TO DO IT LIKE YOU.
SAME HERE.
I WANTED TO BE WITH YOU...
TO SHOW YOU WE COULD SHARE THINGS...
HA! HA! WE'RE KIND OF DUMB...
YES! HEE HEE!
BECAUSE, IN FACT, IF WE HADN'T CHANGED PLACES...
WE'D HAVE BEEN TOGETHER.
SO LET'S JUST START OVER AGAIN.
HERE GOES!
I FEEL LIKE I MADE A MISTAKE AGAIN SOMEWHERE.

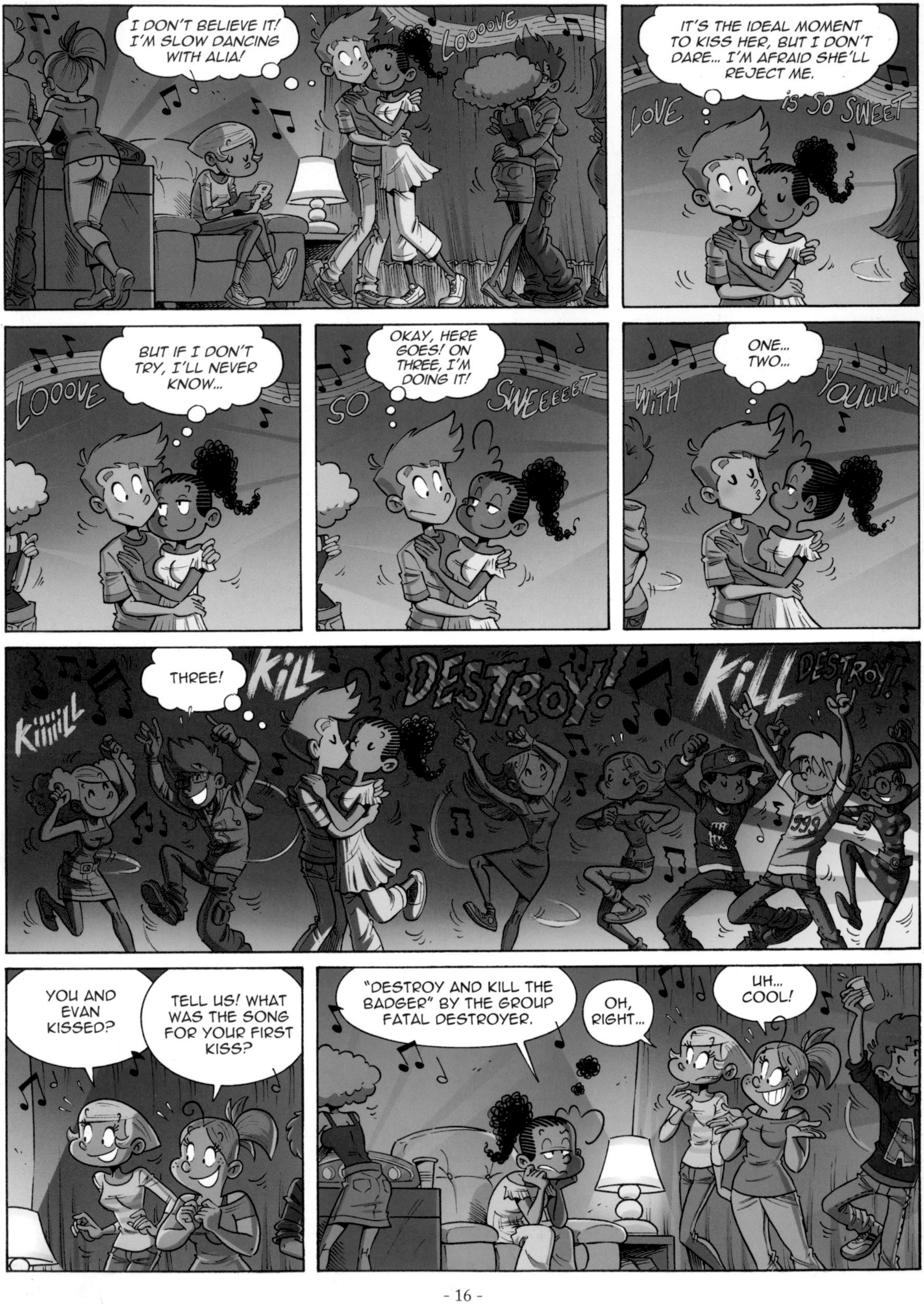
I DON'T BELIEVE IT! I'M SLOW DANCING WITH ALIA!
LOOOOVE
IT'S THE IDEAL MOMENT TO KISS HER, BUT I DON'T DARE... I'M AFRAID SHE'LL REJECT ME.
LOVE
is SO SWEET
BUT IF I DON'T TRY, I'LL NEVER KNOW...
LOOOVE
OKAY, HERE GOES! ON THREE, I'M DOING IT!
SO
SWEEEEEET
ONE... TWO...
WITH
YOUUUU!
THREE!
KIIIIILL
KILL
DESTROY!
KILL
DESTROY!
YOU AND EVAN KISSED?
TELL US! WHAT WAS THE SONG FOR YOUR FIRST KISS?
"DESTROY AND KILL THE BADGER" BY THE GROUP FATAL DESTROYER.
OH, RIGHT...
UH... COOL!

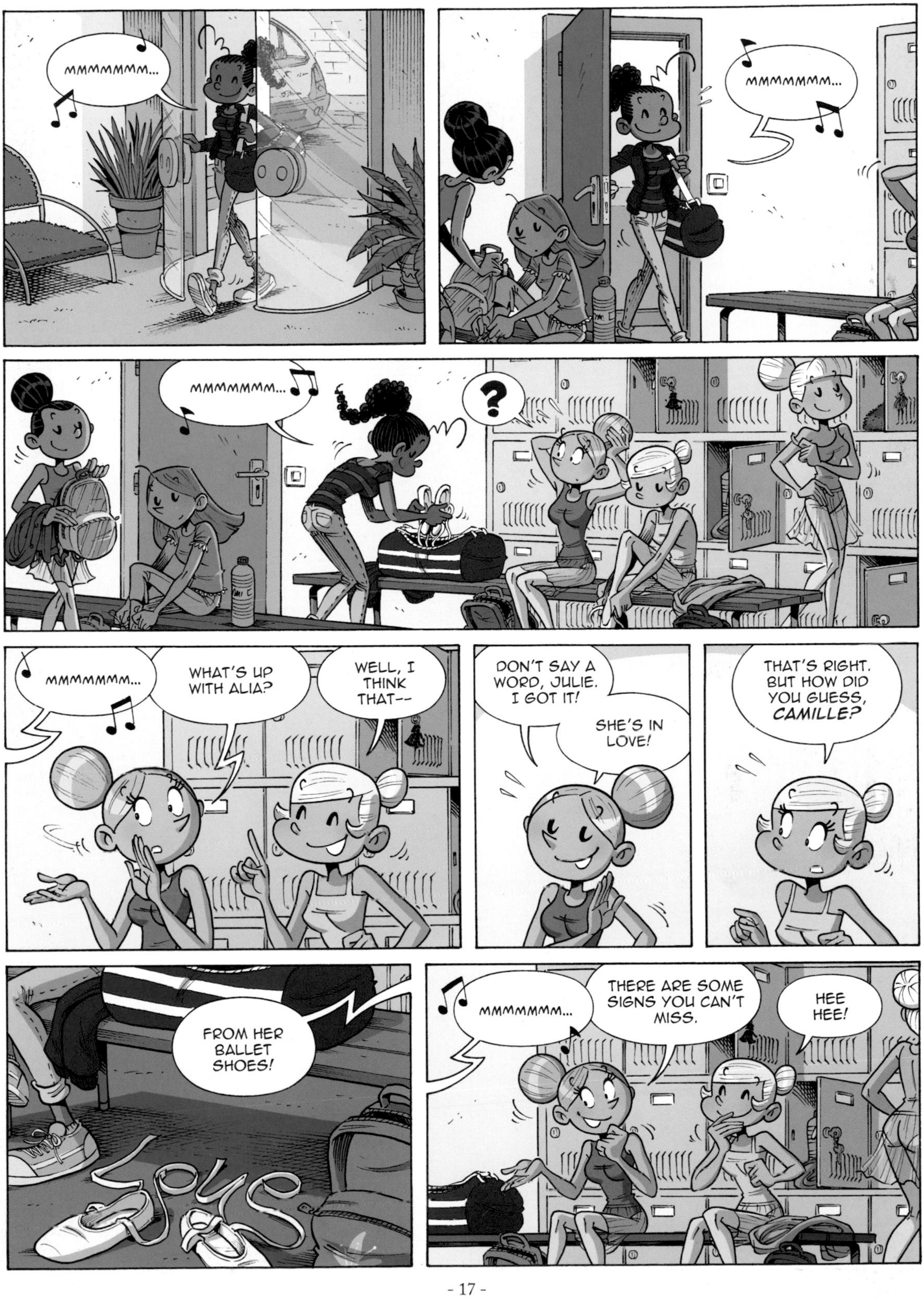
MMMMMMM...
MMMMMMM...
MMMMMMM...
?
MMMMMMM...
WHAT'S UP WITH ALIA?
WELL, I THINK THAT--
DON'T SAY A WORD, JULIE. I GOT IT!
SHE'S IN LOVE!
THAT'S RIGHT. BUT HOW DID YOU GUESS, *CAMILLE?*
FROM HER BALLET SHOES!
MMMMMMM...
THERE ARE SOME SIGNS YOU CAN'T MISS.
HEE HEE!

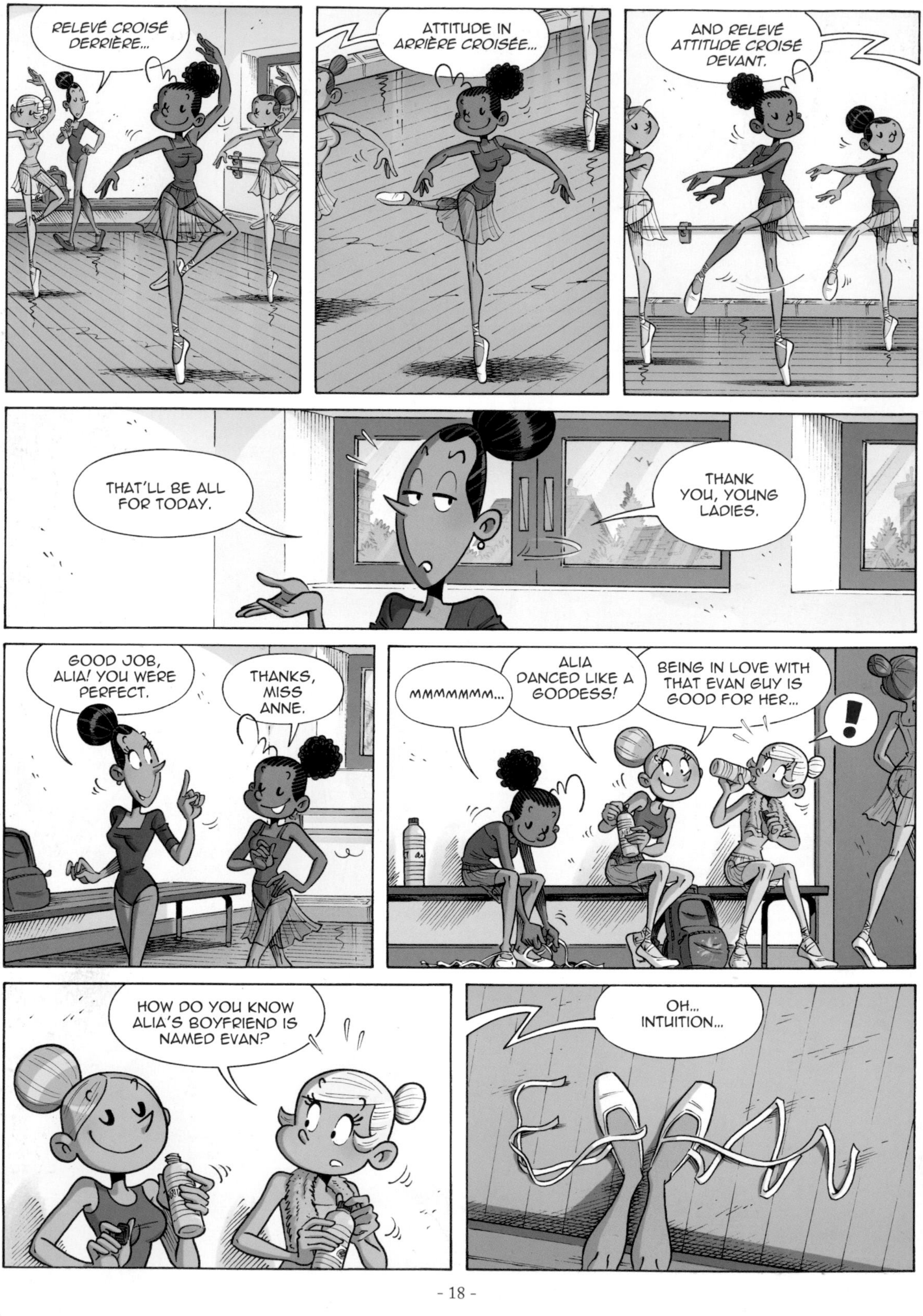
RELEVÉ CROISÉ DERRIÈRE...
ATTITUDE IN ARRIÈRE CROISÉE...
AND RELEVÉ ATTITUDE CROISÉ DEVANT.
THAT'LL BE ALL FOR TODAY.
THANK YOU, YOUNG LADIES.
GOOD JOB, ALIA! YOU WERE PERFECT.
THANKS, MISS ANNE.
MMMMMMM...
ALIA DANCED LIKE A GODDESS!
BEING IN LOVE WITH THAT EVAN GUY IS GOOD FOR HER...
!
HOW DO YOU KNOW ALIA'S BOYFRIEND IS NAMED EVAN?
OH... INTUITION...
EVAN

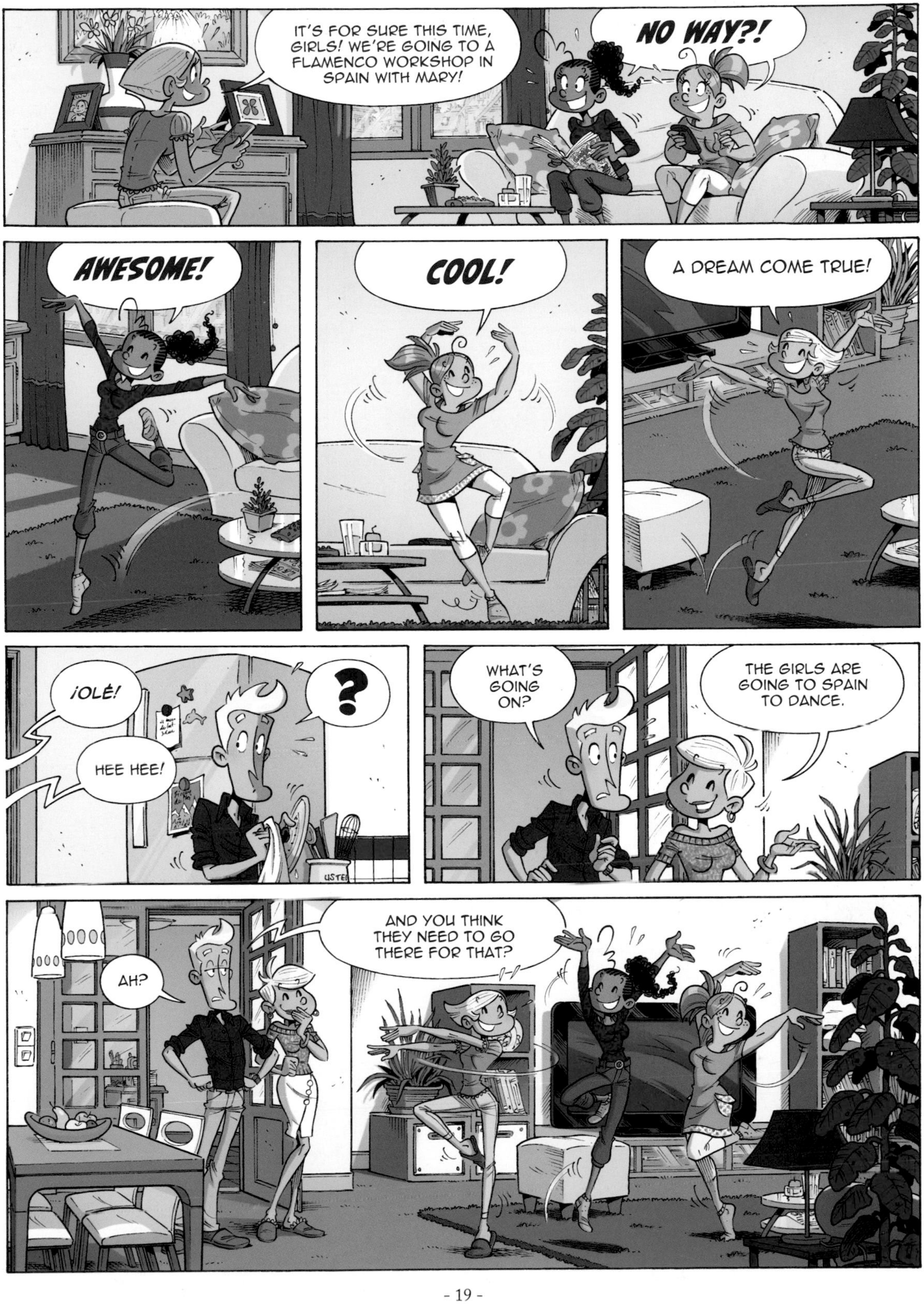
IT'S FOR SURE THIS TIME, GIRLS! WE'RE GOING TO A FLAMENCO WORKSHOP IN SPAIN WITH MARY!
NO WAY?!
AWESOME!
COOL!
A DREAM COME TRUE!
¡OLÉ!
HEE HEE!
?
WHAT'S GOING ON?
THE GIRLS ARE GOING TO SPAIN TO DANCE.
AH?
AND YOU THINK THEY NEED TO GO THERE FOR THAT?

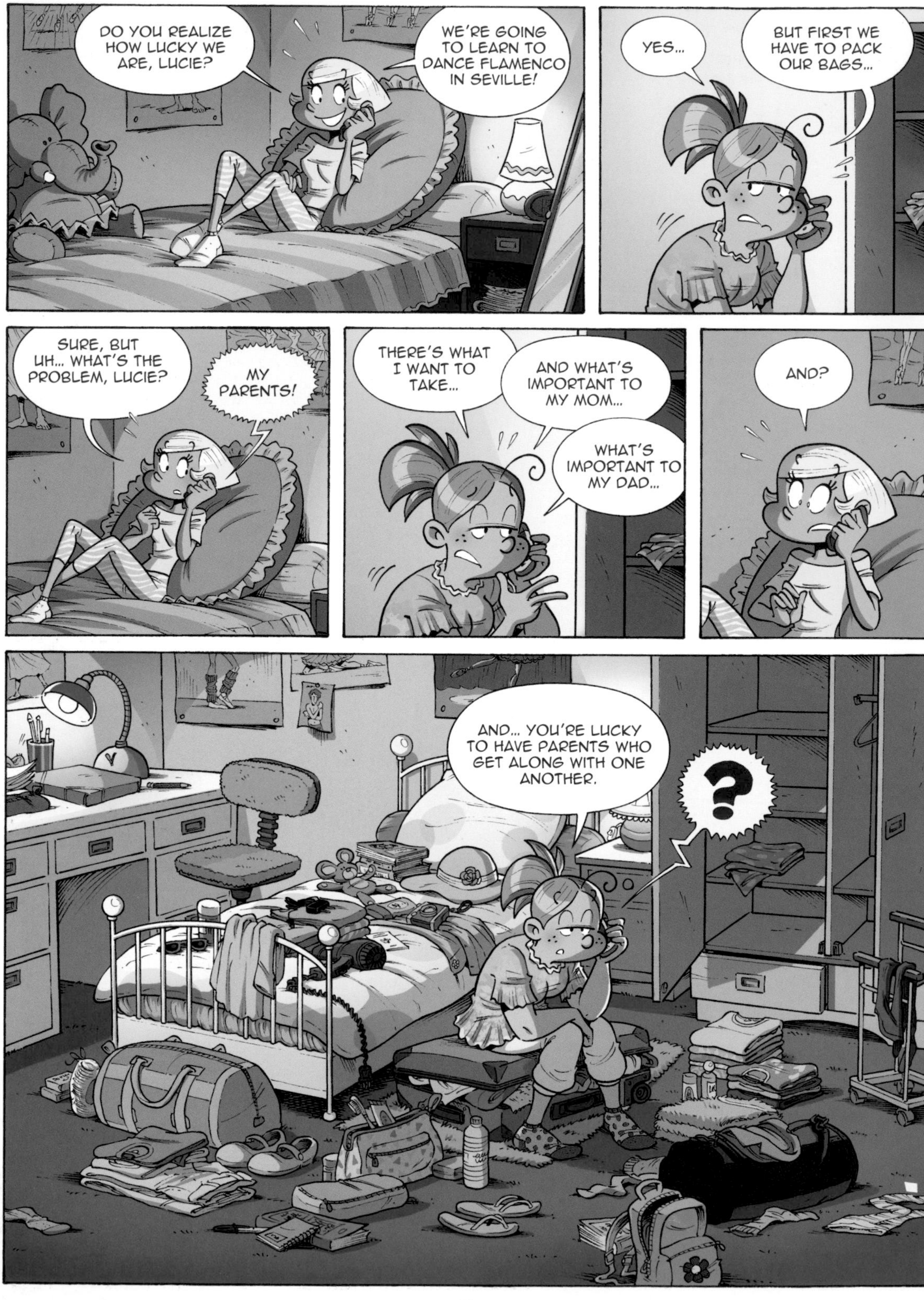

DO YOU REALIZE HOW LUCKY WE ARE, LUCIE?
WE'RE GOING TO LEARN TO DANCE FLAMENCO IN SEVILLE!
YES...
BUT FIRST WE HAVE TO PACK OUR BAGS...
SURE, BUT UH... WHAT'S THE PROBLEM, LUCIE?
MY PARENTS!
THERE'S WHAT I WANT TO TAKE...
AND WHAT'S IMPORTANT TO MY MOM...
WHAT'S IMPORTANT TO MY DAD...
AND?
AND... YOU'RE LUCKY TO HAVE PARENTS WHO GET ALONG WITH ONE ANOTHER.
?

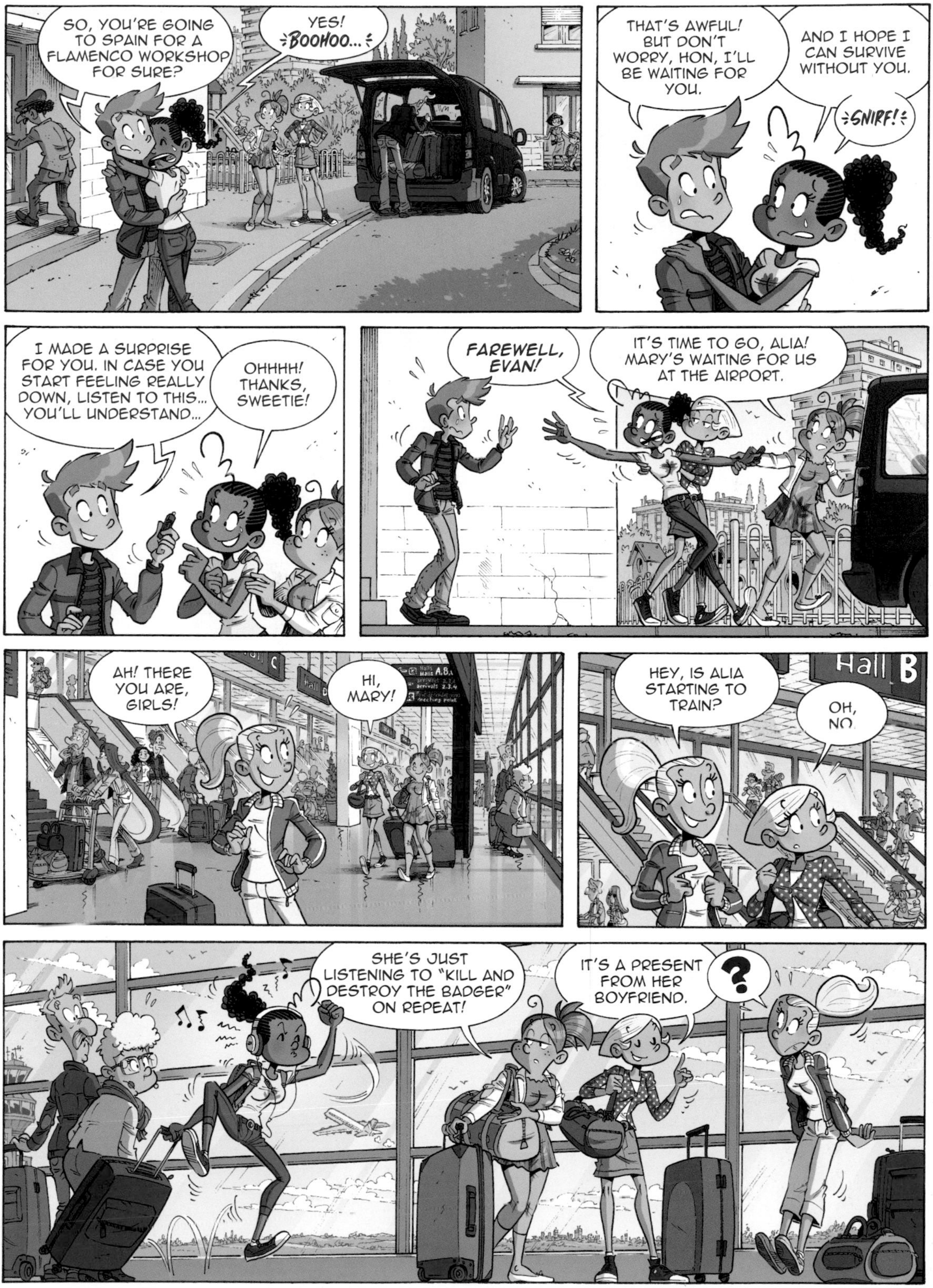
SO, YOU'RE GOING TO SPAIN FOR A FLAMENCO WORKSHOP FOR SURE?
YES! BOOHOO...
THAT'S AWFUL! BUT DON'T WORRY, HON, I'LL BE WAITING FOR YOU.
AND I HOPE I CAN SURVIVE WITHOUT YOU.
SNIRF!
I MADE A SURPRISE FOR YOU. IN CASE YOU START FEELING REALLY DOWN, LISTEN TO THIS... YOU'LL UNDERSTAND...
OHHHH! THANKS, SWEETIE!
FAREWELL, EVAN!
IT'S TIME TO GO, ALIA! MARY'S WAITING FOR US AT THE AIRPORT.
AH! THERE YOU ARE, GIRLS!
HI, MARY!
Hall B
HEY, IS ALIA STARTING TO TRAIN?
OH, NO.
SHE'S JUST LISTENING TO "KILL AND DESTROY THE BADGER" ON REPEAT!
IT'S A PRESENT FROM HER BOYFRIEND.
?

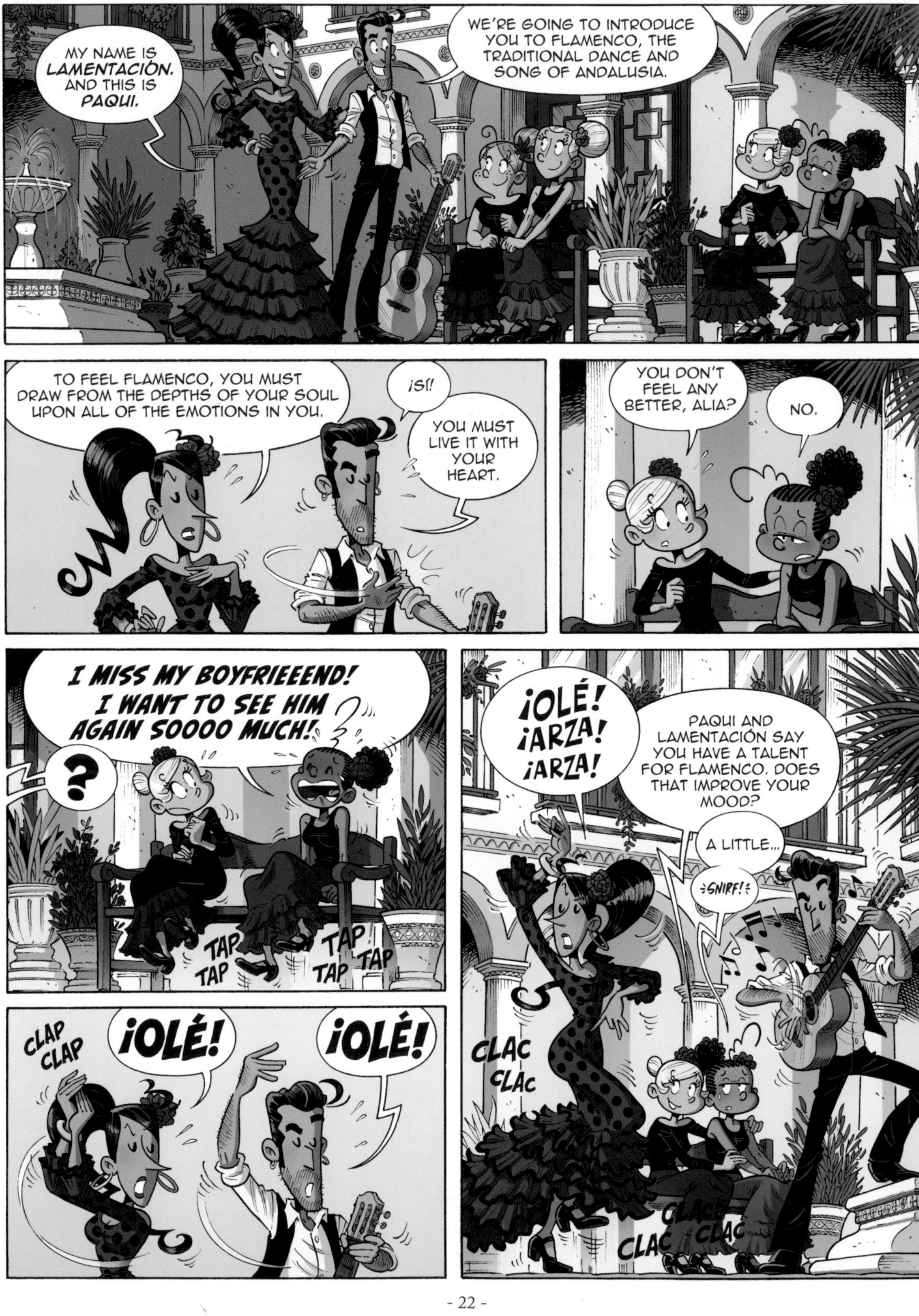
MY NAME IS LAMENTACIÓN. AND THIS IS PAQUI.
WE'RE GOING TO INTRODUCE YOU TO FLAMENCO, THE TRADITIONAL DANCE AND SONG OF ANDALUSIA.
TO FEEL FLAMENCO, YOU MUST DRAW FROM THE DEPTHS OF YOUR SOUL UPON ALL OF THE EMOTIONS IN YOU.
¡SÍ!
YOU MUST LIVE IT WITH YOUR HEART.
YOU DON'T FEEL ANY BETTER, ALIA?
NO.
I MISS MY BOYFRIEEEND! I WANT TO SEE HIM AGAIN SOOOO MUCH!
?
TAP TAP
TAP TAP TAP
CLAP CLAP
¡OLÉ!
¡OLÉ!
¡OLÉ! ¡ARZA! ¡ARZA!
PAQUI AND LAMENTACIÓN SAY YOU HAVE A TALENT FOR FLAMENCO. DOES THAT IMPROVE YOUR MOOD?
A LITTLE...
SNIRF!
CLAC CLAC
CLAC CLAC CLAC

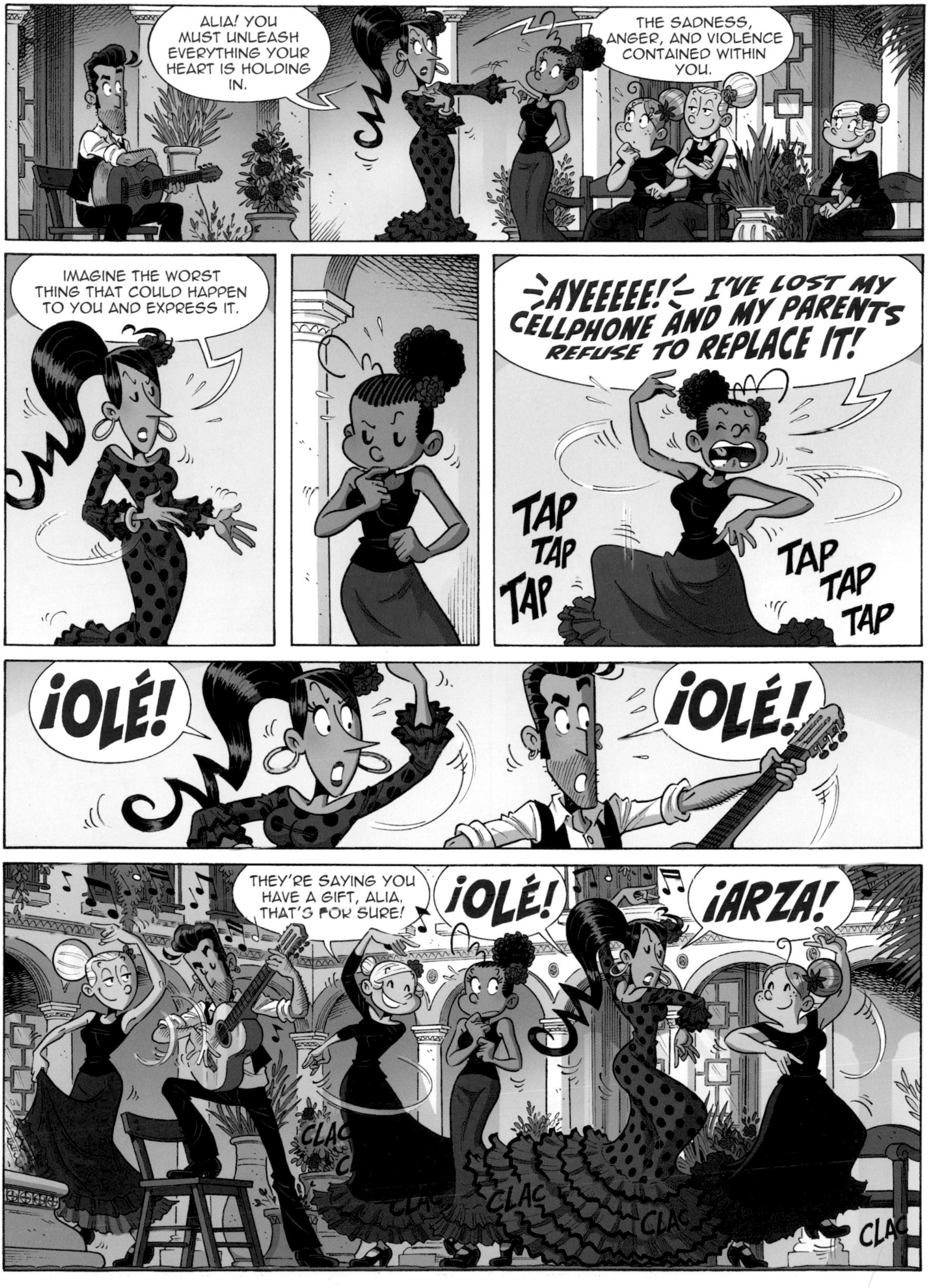
ALIA! YOU MUST UNLEASH EVERYTHING YOUR HEART IS HOLDING IN.
THE SADNESS, ANGER, AND VIOLENCE CONTAINED WITHIN YOU.
IMAGINE THE WORST THING THAT COULD HAPPEN TO YOU AND EXPRESS IT.
AYEEEEE! I'VE LOST MY CELLPHONE AND MY PARENTS REFUSE TO REPLACE IT!
TAP TAP TAP
TAP TAP TAP
¡OLÉ!
¡OLÉ!
THEY'RE SAYING YOU HAVE A GIFT, ALIA, THAT'S FOR SURE!
¡OLÉ!
¡ARZA!
CLAC
CLAC
CLAC
CLAC
CLAC

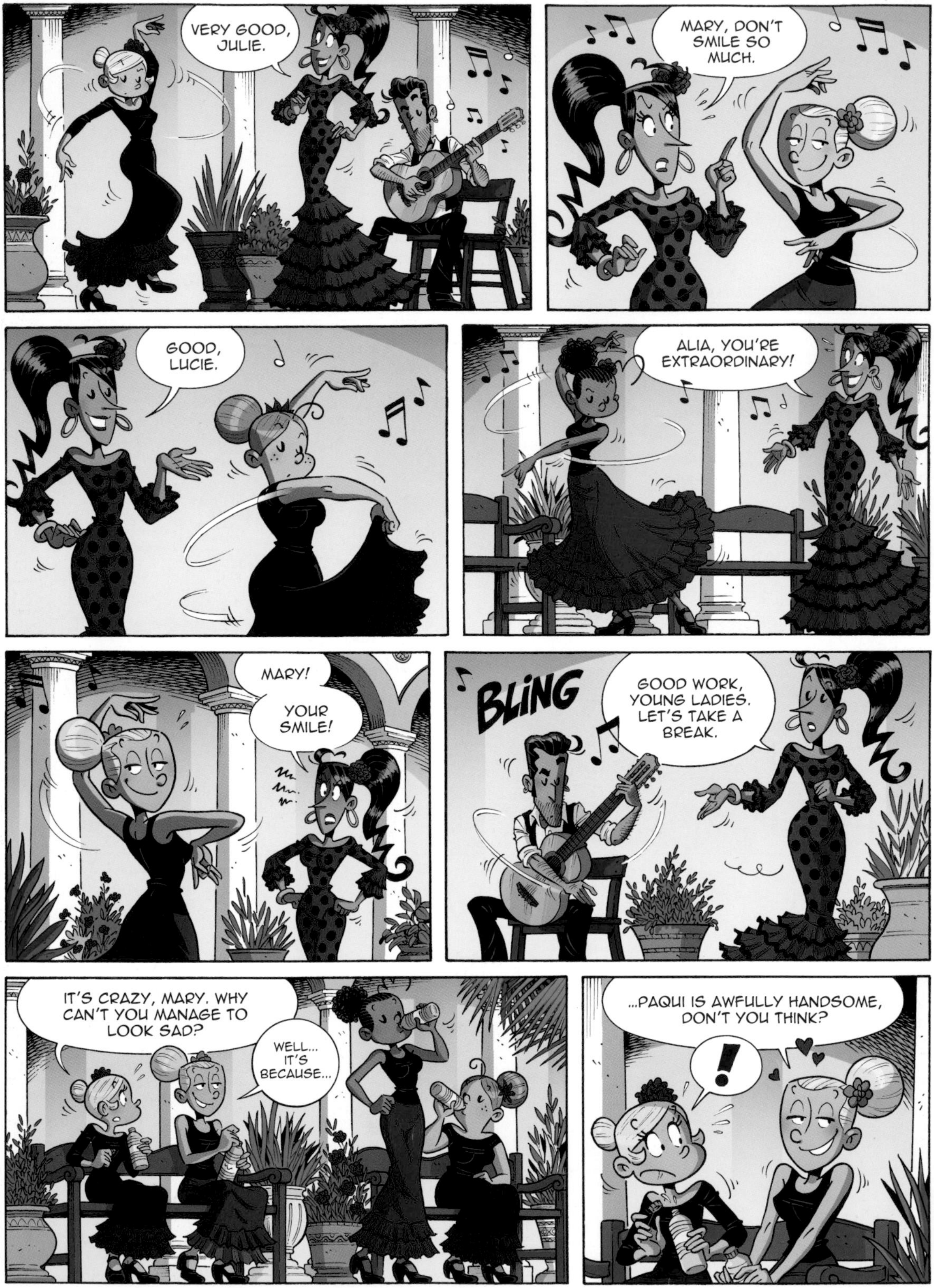
VERY GOOD, JULIE.
MARY, DON'T SMILE SO MUCH.
GOOD, LUCIE.
ALIA, YOU'RE EXTRAORDINARY!
MARY!
YOUR SMILE!
BLING
GOOD WORK, YOUNG LADIES. LET'S TAKE A BREAK.
IT'S CRAZY, MARY. WHY CAN'T YOU MANAGE TO LOOK SAD?
WELL... IT'S BECAUSE...
...PAQUI IS AWFULLY HANDSOME, DON'T YOU THINK?
!

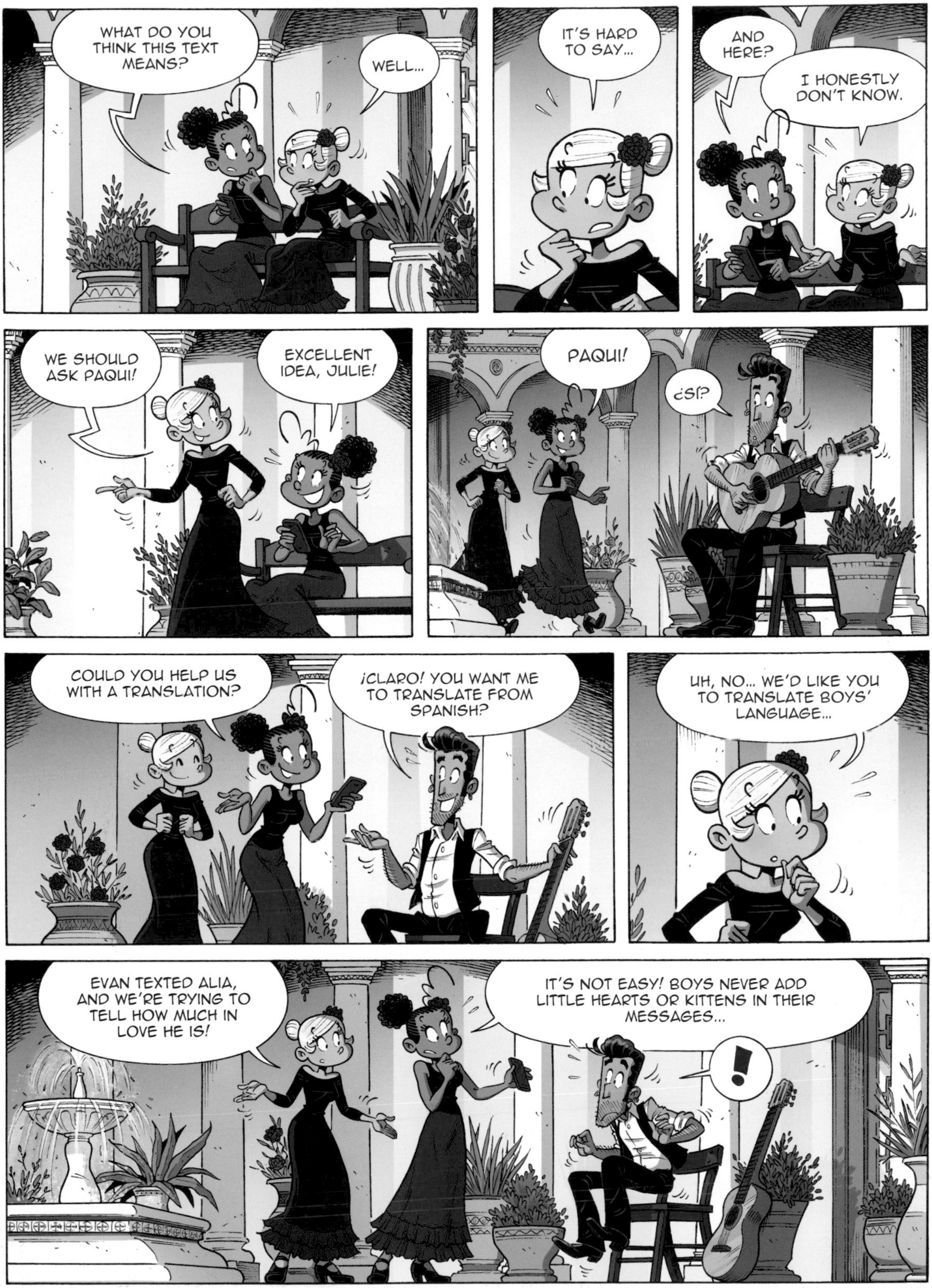
WHAT DO YOU THINK THIS TEXT MEANS?
WELL...
IT'S HARD TO SAY...
AND HERE?
I HONESTLY DON'T KNOW.
WE SHOULD ASK PAQUI!
EXCELLENT IDEA, JULIE!
PAQUI!
¿SI?
COULD YOU HELP US WITH A TRANSLATION?
¡CLARO! YOU WANT ME TO TRANSLATE FROM SPANISH?
UH, NO... WE'D LIKE YOU TO TRANSLATE BOYS' LANGUAGE...
EVAN TEXTED ALIA, AND WE'RE TRYING TO TELL HOW MUCH IN LOVE HE IS!
IT'S NOT EASY! BOYS NEVER ADD LITTLE HEARTS OR KITTENS IN THEIR MESSAGES...
!

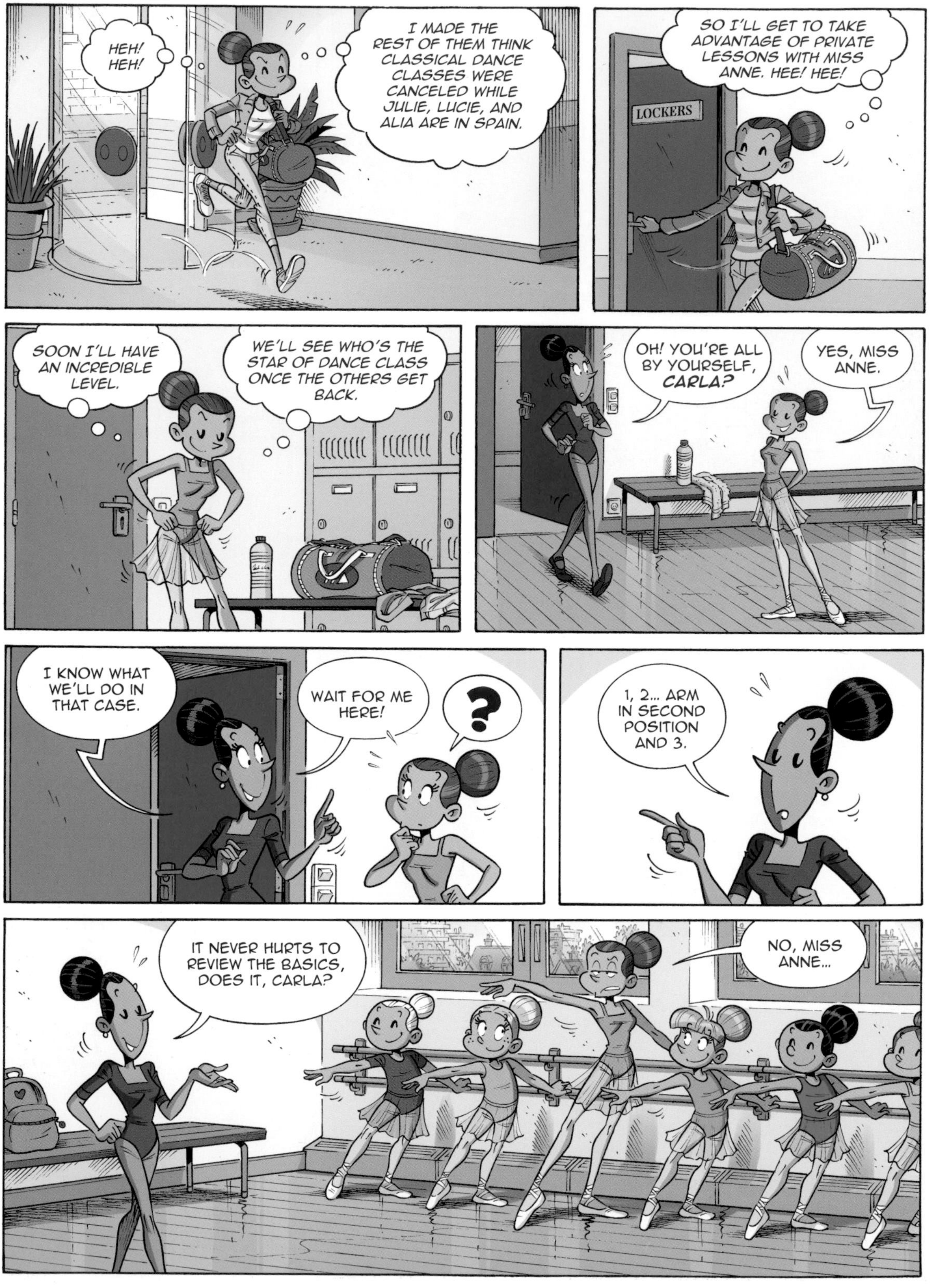
HEH! HEH!
I MADE THE REST OF THEM THINK CLASSICAL DANCE CLASSES WERE CANCELED WHILE JULIE, LUCIE, AND ALIA ARE IN SPAIN.
SO I'LL GET TO TAKE ADVANTAGE OF PRIVATE LESSONS WITH MISS ANNE. HEE! HEE!
LOCKERS
SOON I'LL HAVE AN INCREDIBLE LEVEL.
WE'LL SEE WHO'S THE STAR OF DANCE CLASS ONCE THE OTHERS GET BACK.
OH! YOU'RE ALL BY YOURSELF, CARLA?
YES, MISS ANNE.
I KNOW WHAT WE'LL DO IN THAT CASE.
WAIT FOR ME HERE!
?
1, 2... ARM IN SECOND POSITION AND 3.
IT NEVER HURTS TO REVIEW THE BASICS, DOES IT, CARLA?
NO, MISS ANNE...

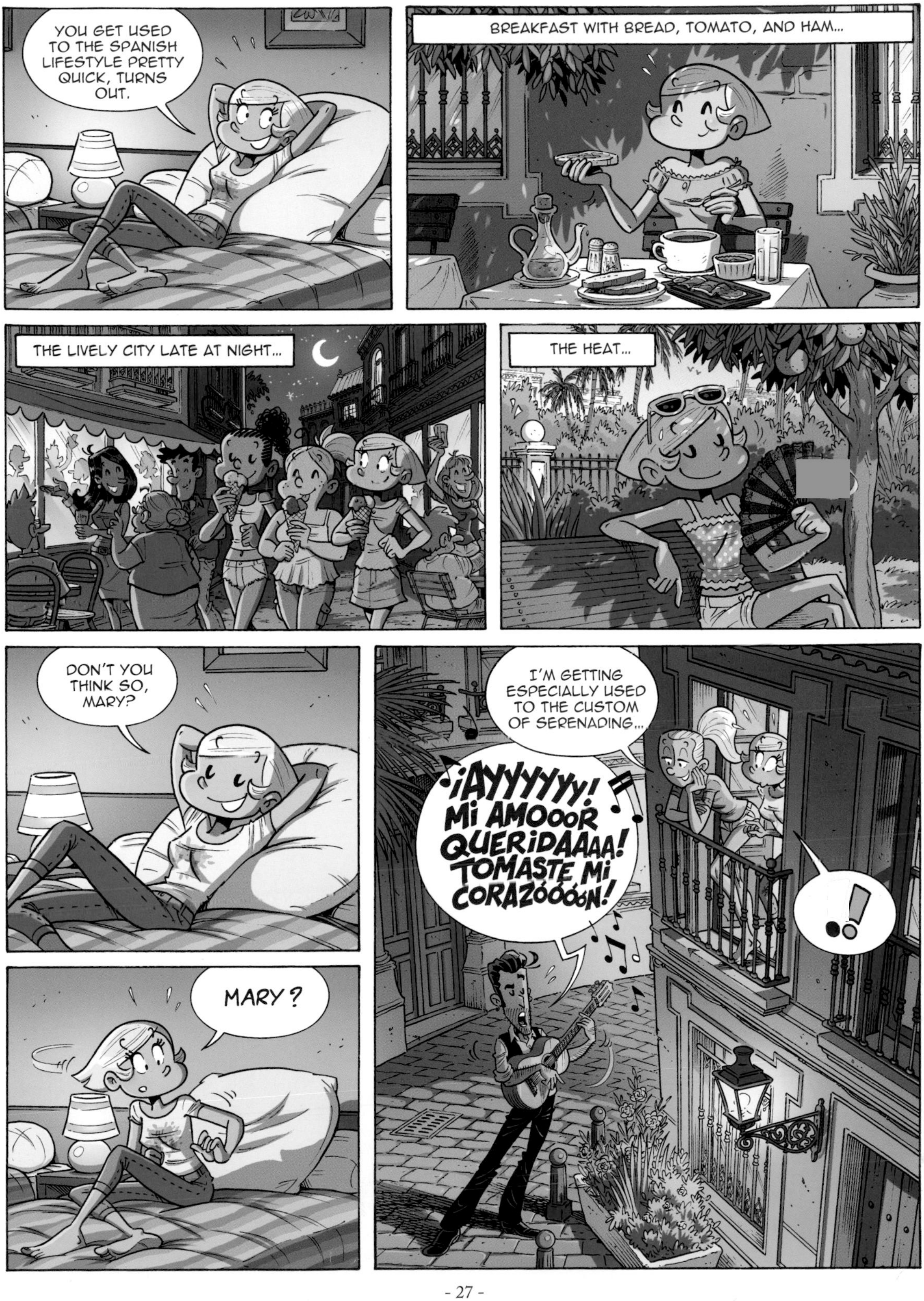
YOU GET USED TO THE SPANISH LIFESTYLE PRETTY QUICK, TURNS OUT.
BREAKFAST WITH BREAD, TOMATO, AND HAM...
THE LIVELY CITY LATE AT NIGHT...
THE HEAT...
DON'T YOU THINK SO, MARY?
I'M GETTING ESPECIALLY USED TO THE CUSTOM OF SERENADING...
¡AYYYYYY! MI AMOOOR QUERIDAAAA! TOMASTE MI CORAZÓÓÓÓÓN!
MARY ?
!

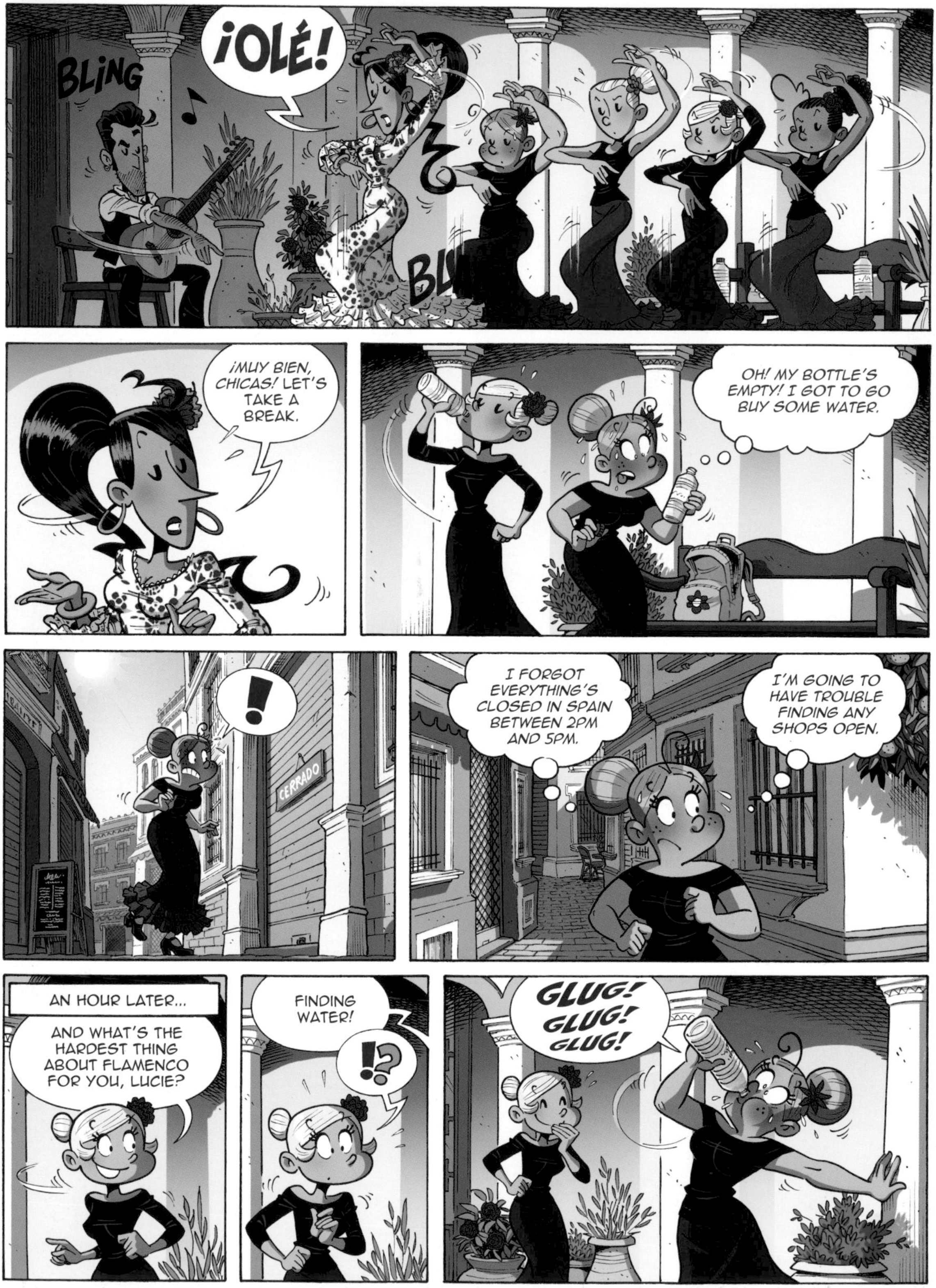

BLING
¡OLÉ!
BLING
¡MUY BIEN, CHICAS! LET'S TAKE A BREAK.
OH! MY BOTTLE'S EMPTY! I GOT TO GO BUY SOME WATER.
!
CERRADO
I FORGOT EVERYTHING'S CLOSED IN SPAIN BETWEEN 2PM AND 5PM.
I'M GOING TO HAVE TROUBLE FINDING ANY SHOPS OPEN.
AN HOUR LATER...
AND WHAT'S THE HARDEST THING ABOUT FLAMENCO FOR YOU, LUCIE?
FINDING WATER!
!?
GLUG! GLUG! GLUG!

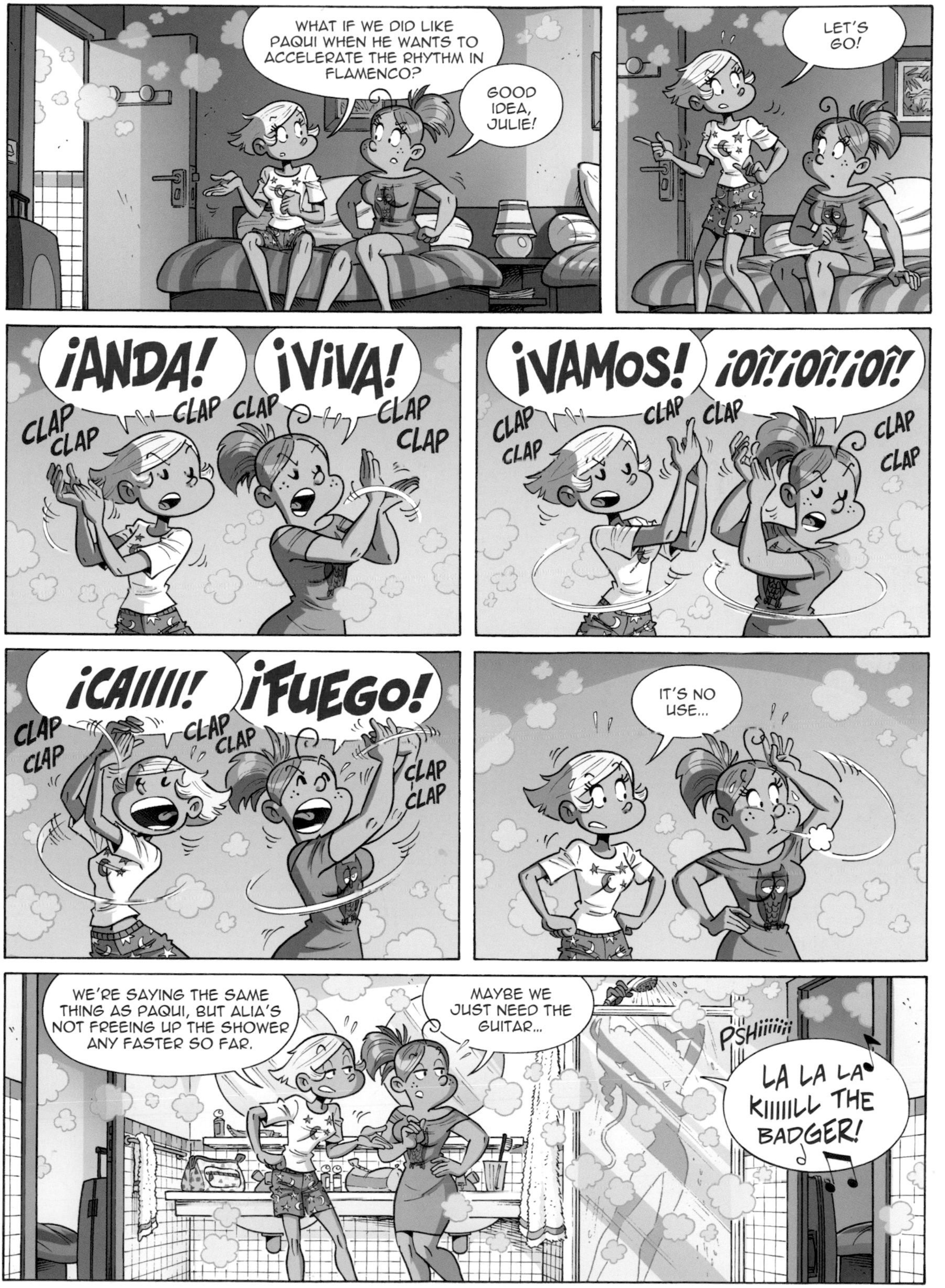
WHAT IF WE DID LIKE PAQUI WHEN HE WANTS TO ACCELERATE THE RHYTHM IN FLAMENCO?
GOOD IDEA, JULIE!
LET'S GO!
¡ANDA!
CLAP CLAP
CLAP
CLAP
¡VIVA!
CLAP CLAP
¡VAMOS!
CLAP CLAP
CLAP
CLAP
¡OÎ!¡OÎ!¡OÎ!
CLAP CLAP
¡CAIIII!
CLAP CLAP
CLAP CLAP
¡FUEGO!
CLAP CLAP
IT'S NO USE...
WE'RE SAYING THE SAME THING AS PAQUI, BUT ALIA'S NOT FREEING UP THE SHOWER ANY FASTER SO FAR.
MAYBE WE JUST NEED THE GUITAR...
PSHiiiiiii
LA LA LA KIIIIILL THE BADGER!

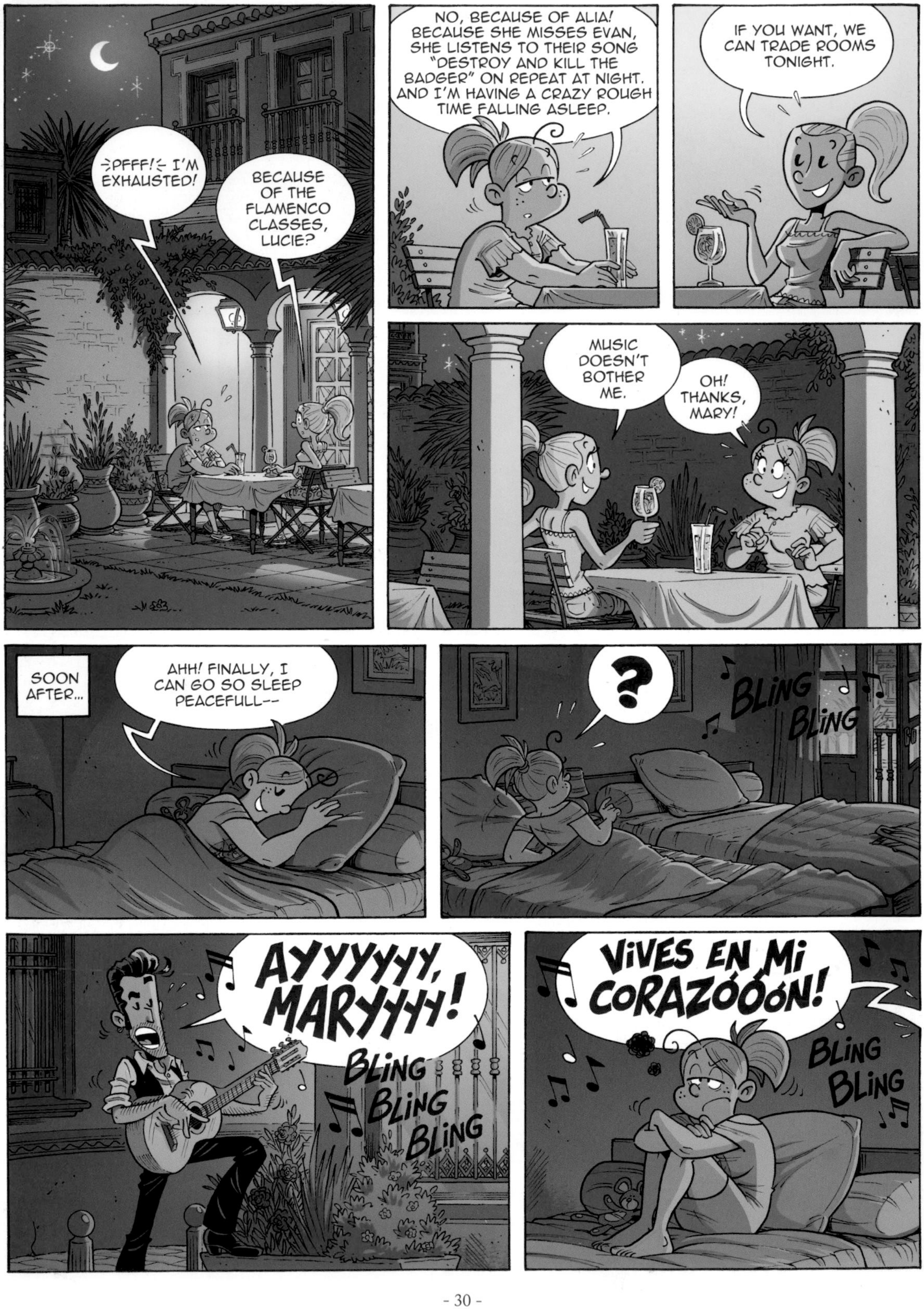

PFFF! I'M EXHAUSTED!
BECAUSE OF THE FLAMENCO CLASSES, LUCIE?
NO, BECAUSE OF ALIA! BECAUSE SHE MISSES EVAN, SHE LISTENS TO THEIR SONG "DESTROY AND KILL THE BADGER" ON REPEAT AT NIGHT. AND I'M HAVING A CRAZY ROUGH TIME FALLING ASLEEP.
IF YOU WANT, WE CAN TRADE ROOMS TONIGHT.
MUSIC DOESN'T BOTHER ME.
OH! THANKS, MARY!
SOON AFTER...
AHH! FINALLY, I CAN GO SO SLEEP PEACEFULL--
?
BLING BLING
AYYYYY, MARYYYY!
BLING BLING BLING
VIVES EN MI CORAZÓÓÓN!
BLING BLING

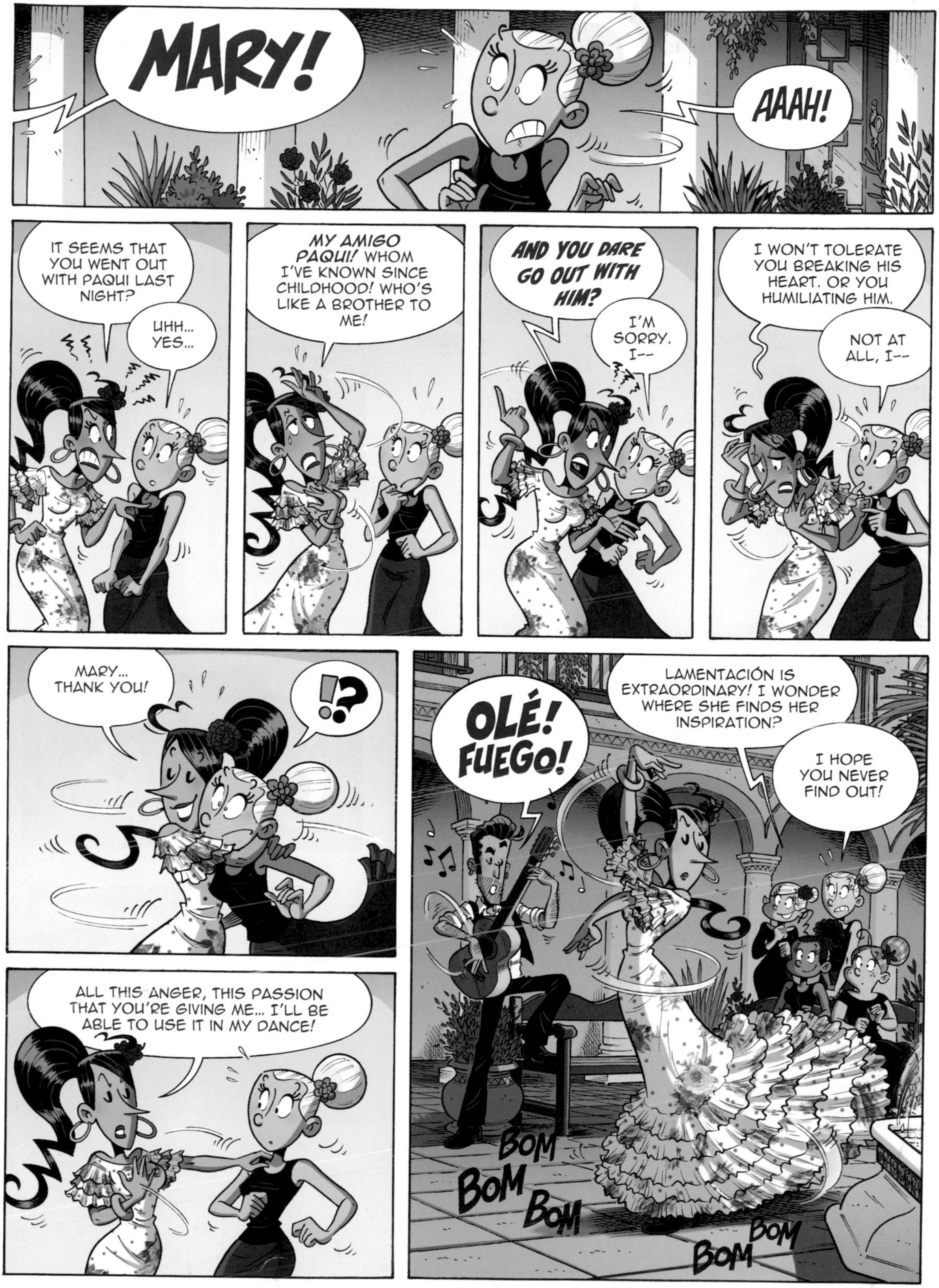
MARY!
AAAH!
IT SEEMS THAT YOU WENT OUT WITH PAQUI LAST NIGHT?
UHH... YES...
MY AMIGO PAQUI! WHOM I'VE KNOWN SINCE CHILDHOOD! WHO'S LIKE A BROTHER TO ME!
AND YOU DARE GO OUT WITH HIM?
I'M SORRY. I--
I WON'T TOLERATE YOU BREAKING HIS HEART. OR YOU HUMILIATING HIM.
NOT AT ALL, I--
MARY... THANK YOU!
!?
ALL THIS ANGER, THIS PASSION THAT YOU'RE GIVING ME... I'LL BE ABLE TO USE IT IN MY DANCE!
OLÉ! FUEGO!
LAMENTACIÓN IS EXTRAORDINARY! I WONDER WHERE SHE FINDS HER INSPIRATION?
I HOPE YOU NEVER FIND OUT!
BOM
BOM
BOM
BOM
BOM

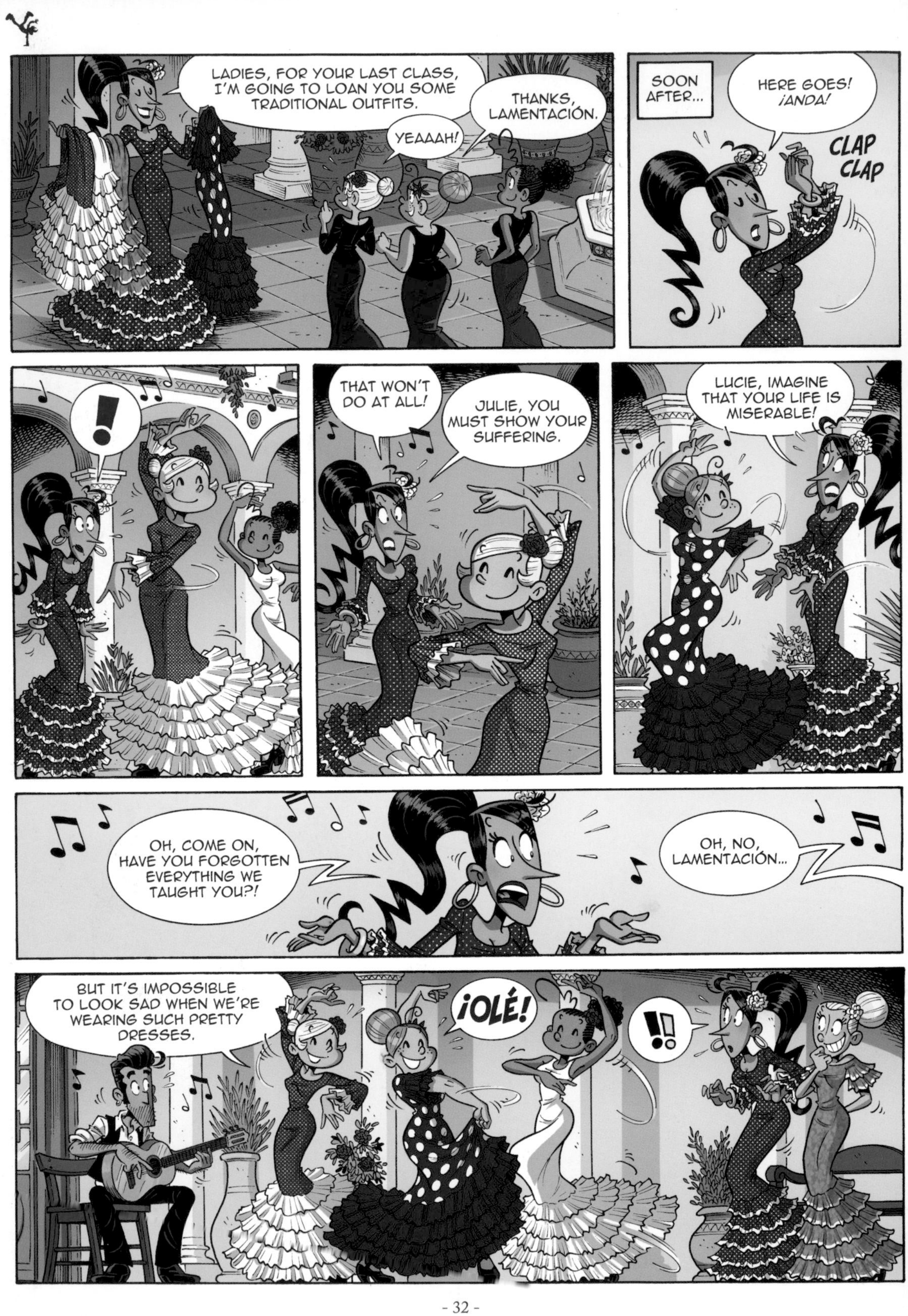
LADIES, FOR YOUR LAST CLASS, I'M GOING TO LOAN YOU SOME TRADITIONAL OUTFITS.
YEAAAH!
THANKS, LAMENTACIÓN.
SOON AFTER...
HERE GOES! ¡ANDA!
CLAP CLAP
!
THAT WON'T DO AT ALL!
JULIE, YOU MUST SHOW YOUR SUFFERING.
LUCIE, IMAGINE THAT YOUR LIFE IS MISERABLE!
OH, COME ON, HAVE YOU FORGOTTEN EVERYTHING WE TAUGHT YOU?!
OH, NO, LAMENTACIÓN...
BUT IT'S IMPOSSIBLE TO LOOK SAD WHEN WE'RE WEARING SUCH PRETTY DRESSES.
¡OLÉ!
!!

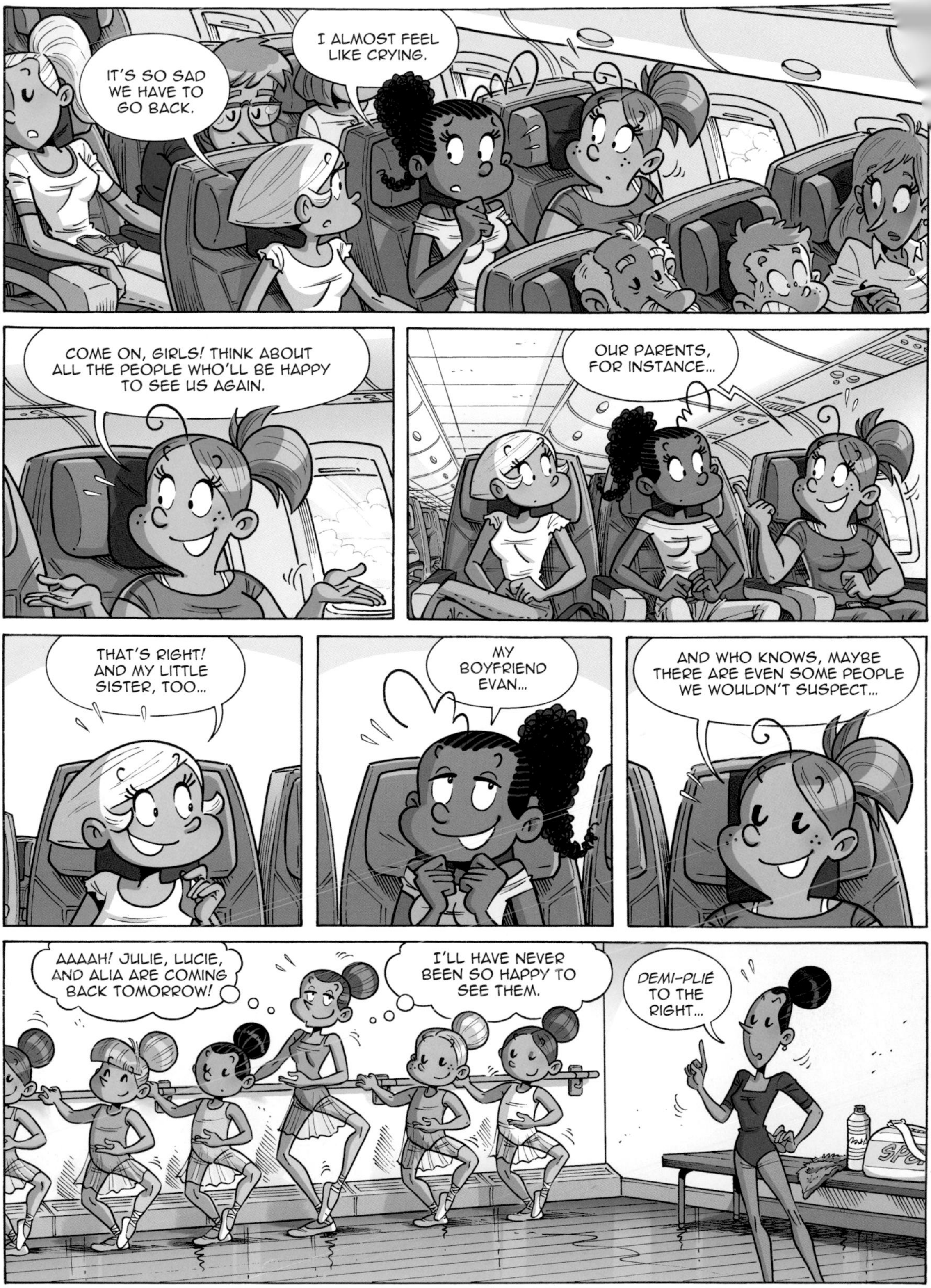
IT'S SO SAD WE HAVE TO GO BACK.
I ALMOST FEEL LIKE CRYING.
COME ON, GIRLS! THINK ABOUT ALL THE PEOPLE WHO'LL BE HAPPY TO SEE US AGAIN.
OUR PARENTS, FOR INSTANCE...
THAT'S RIGHT! AND MY LITTLE SISTER, TOO...
MY BOYFRIEND EVAN...
AND WHO KNOWS, MAYBE THERE ARE EVEN SOME PEOPLE WE WOULDN'T SUSPECT...
AAAAH! JULIE, LUCIE, AND ALIA ARE COMING BACK TOMORROW!
I'LL HAVE NEVER BEEN SO HAPPY TO SEE THEM.
DEMI-PLIÉ TO THE RIGHT...

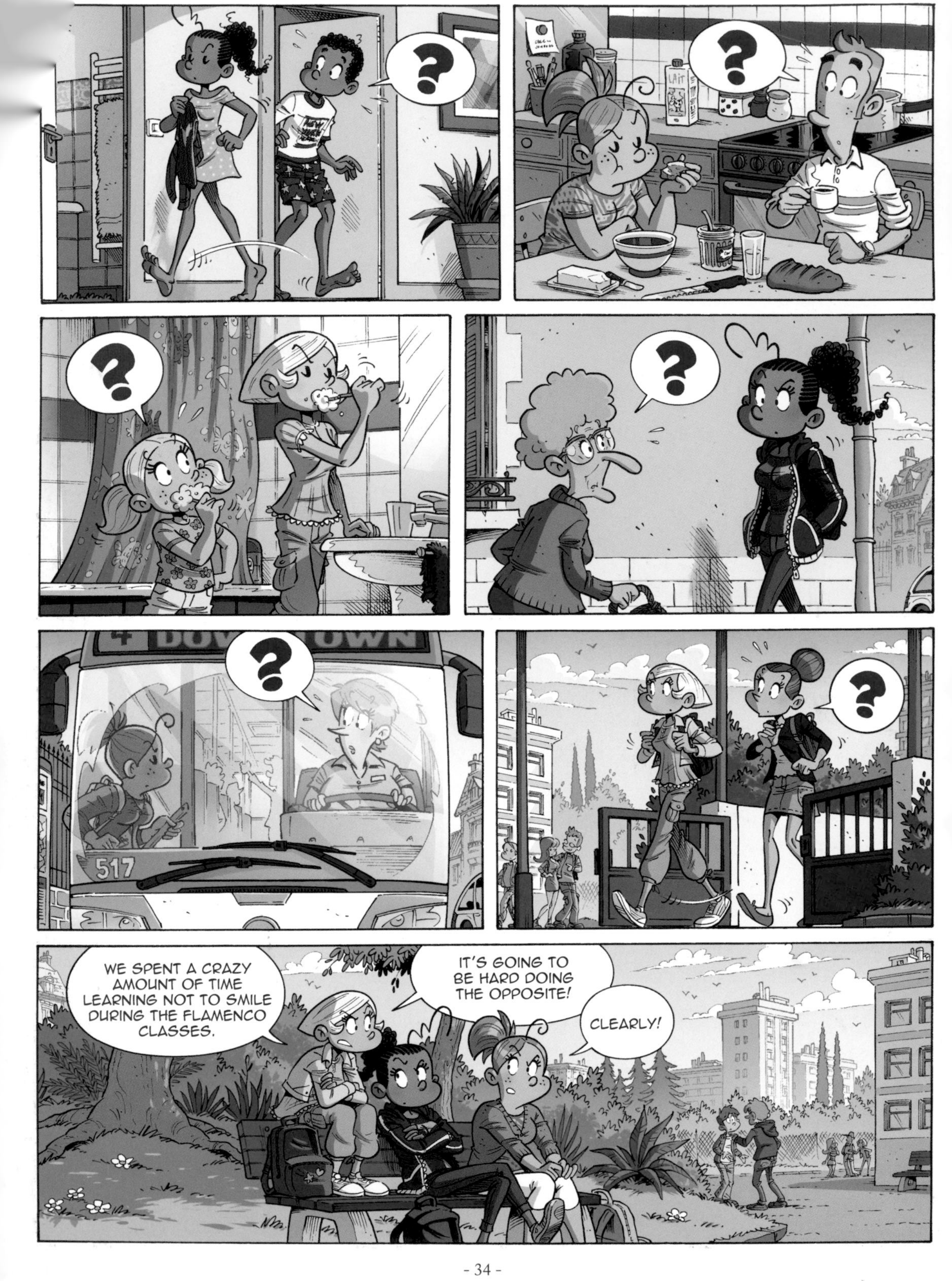
?
?
?
?
?
?
517
WE SPENT A CRAZY AMOUNT OF TIME LEARNING NOT TO SMILE DURING THE FLAMENCO CLASSES.
IT'S GOING TO BE HARD DOING THE OPPOSITE!
CLEARLY!

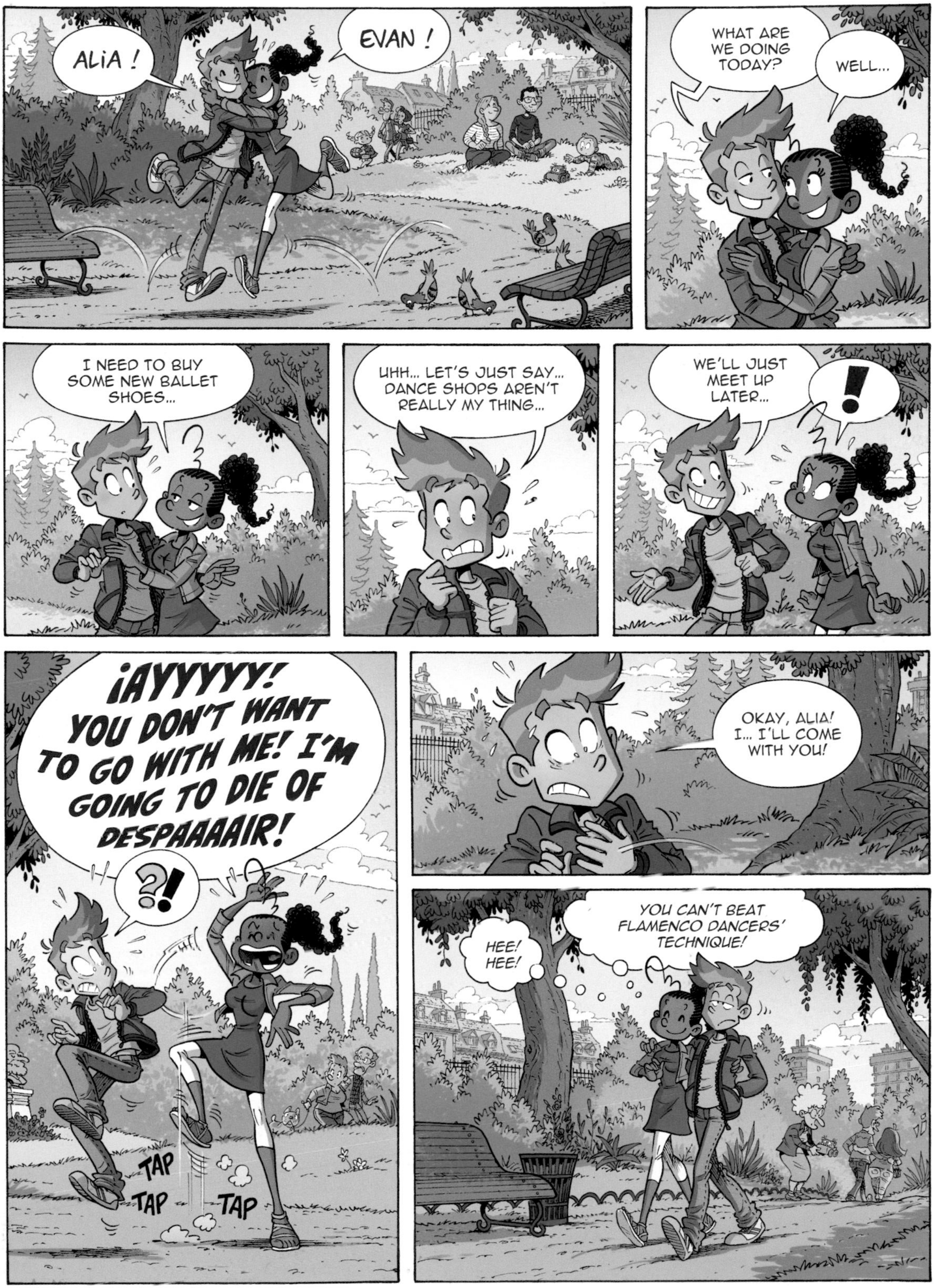
ALiA !
EVAN !
WHAT ARE WE DOING TODAY?
WELL...
I NEED TO BUY SOME NEW BALLET SHOES...
UHH... LET'S JUST SAY... DANCE SHOPS AREN'T REALLY MY THING...
WE'LL JUST MEET UP LATER...
!
¡AYYYYY! YOU DON'T WANT TO GO WITH ME! I'M GOING TO DIE OF DESPAAAAIR!
?!
TAP
TAP
TAP
OKAY, ALIA! I... I'LL COME WITH YOU!
HEE! HEE!
YOU CAN'T BEAT FLAMENCO DANCERS' TECHNIQUE!

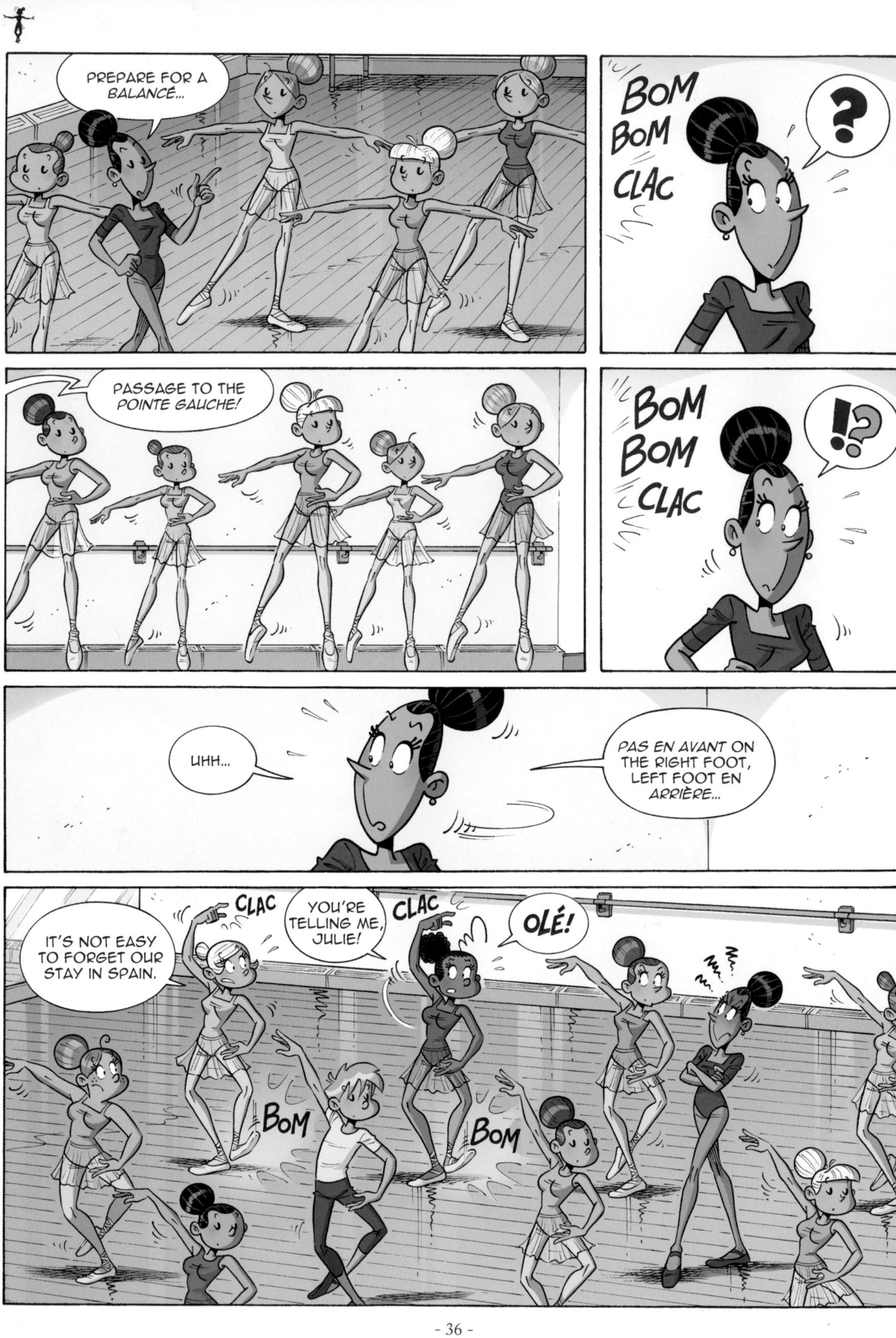
PREPARE FOR A BALANCÉ...
BOM
BOM
CLAC
?
PASSAGE TO THE POINTE GAUCHE!
BOM
BOM
CLAC
!?
UHH...
PAS EN AVANT ON THE RIGHT FOOT, LEFT FOOT EN ARRIÈRE...
IT'S NOT EASY TO FORGET OUR STAY IN SPAIN.
CLAC
YOU'RE TELLING ME, JULIE!
CLAC
OLÉ!
BOM
BOM

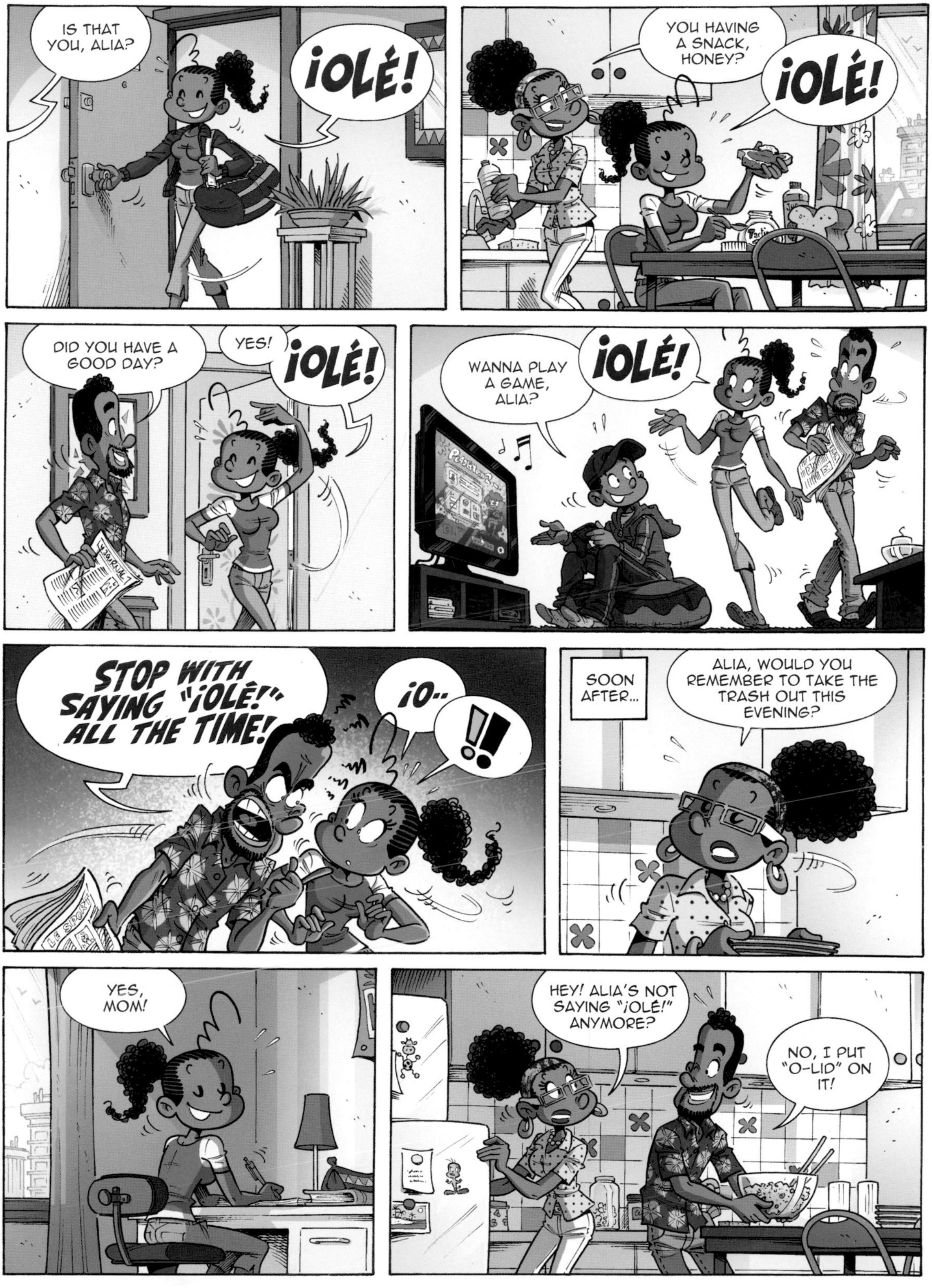
IS THAT YOU, ALIA?
¡OLÉ!
YOU HAVING A SNACK, HONEY?
¡OLÉ!
DID YOU HAVE A GOOD DAY?
YES!
¡OLÉ!
WANNA PLAY A GAME, ALIA?
¡OLÉ!
STOP WITH SAYING "¡OLÉ!" ALL THE TIME!
¡O..
!!
SOON AFTER...
ALIA, WOULD YOU REMEMBER TO TAKE THE TRASH OUT THIS EVENING?
YES, MOM!
HEY! ALIA'S NOT SAYING "¡OLÉ!" ANYMORE?
NO, I PUT "O-LID" ON IT!

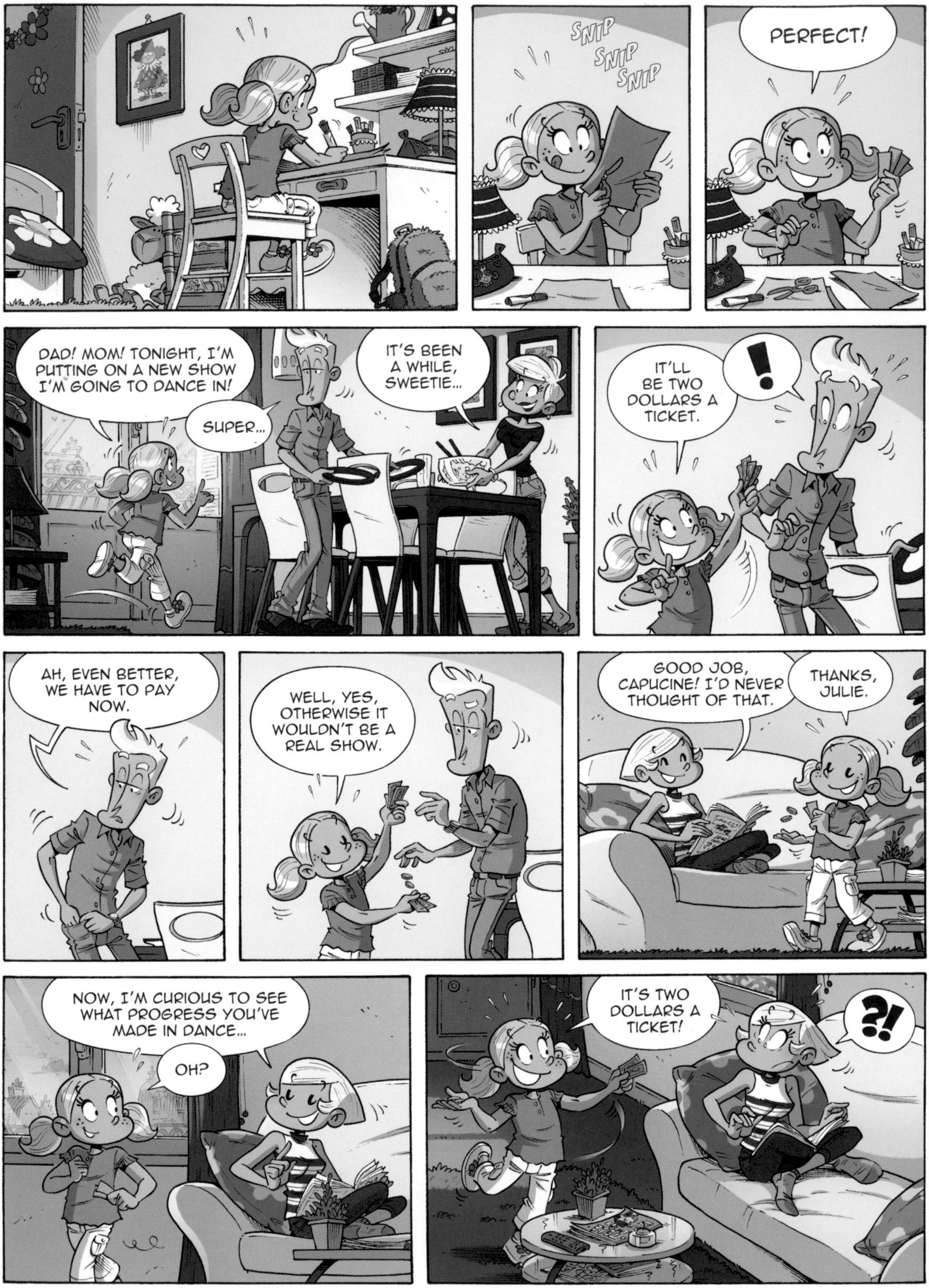

SNIP SNIP SNIP
PERFECT!
DAD! MOM! TONIGHT, I'M PUTTING ON A NEW SHOW I'M GOING TO DANCE IN!
SUPER...
IT'S BEEN A WHILE, SWEETIE...
IT'LL BE TWO DOLLARS A TICKET.
!
AH, EVEN BETTER, WE HAVE TO PAY NOW.
WELL, YES, OTHERWISE IT WOULDN'T BE A REAL SHOW.
GOOD JOB, CAPUCINE! I'D NEVER THOUGHT OF THAT.
THANKS, JULIE.
NOW, I'M CURIOUS TO SEE WHAT PROGRESS YOU'VE MADE IN DANCE...
OH?
IT'S TWO DOLLARS A TICKET!
?!

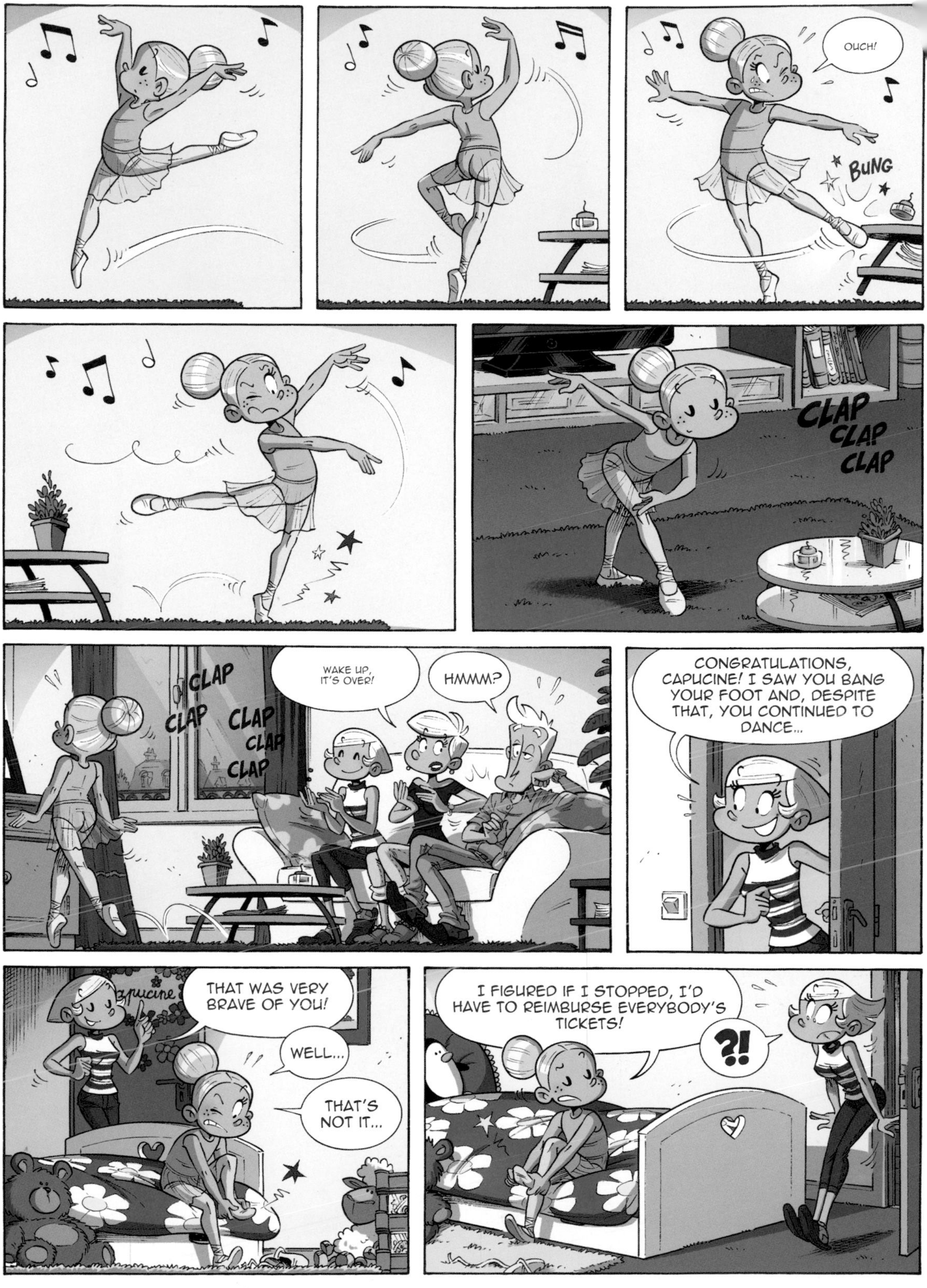
OUCH!
BUNG
CLAP
CLAP
CLAP
CLAP
CLAP
CLAP
CLAP
CLAP
WAKE UP, IT'S OVER!
HMMM?
CONGRATULATIONS, CAPUCINE! I SAW YOU BANG YOUR FOOT AND, DESPITE THAT, YOU CONTINUED TO DANCE...
THAT WAS VERY BRAVE OF YOU!
WELL...
THAT'S NOT IT...
I FIGURED IF I STOPPED, I'D HAVE TO REIMBURSE EVERYBODY'S TICKETS!
?!

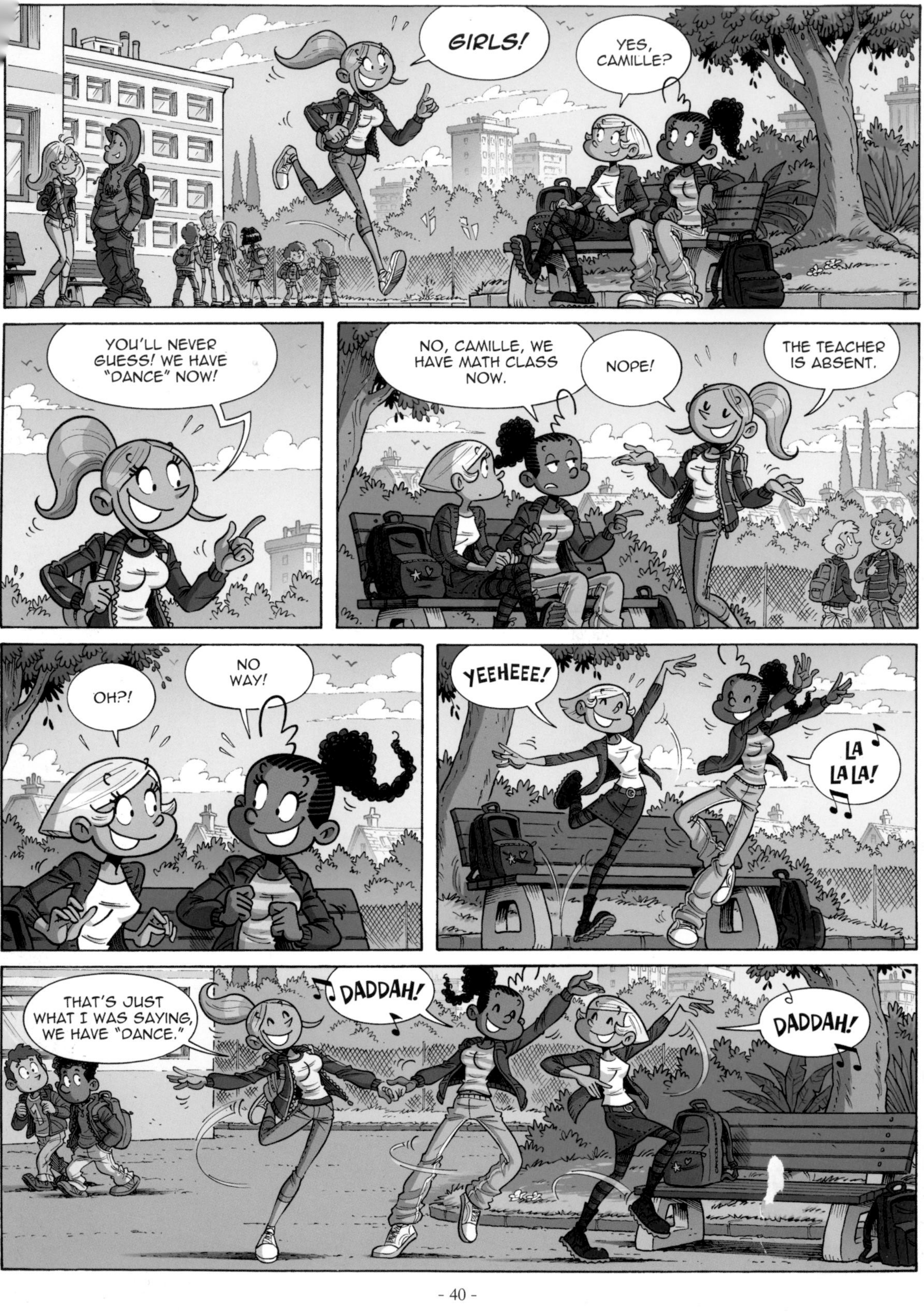
GIRLS!
YES, CAMILLE?
YOU'LL NEVER GUESS! WE HAVE "DANCE" NOW!
NO, CAMILLE, WE HAVE MATH CLASS NOW.
NOPE!
THE TEACHER IS ABSENT.
OH?!
NO WAY!
YEEHEEE!
LA LA LA!
THAT'S JUST WHAT I WAS SAYING, WE HAVE "DANCE."
DADDAH!
DADDAH!

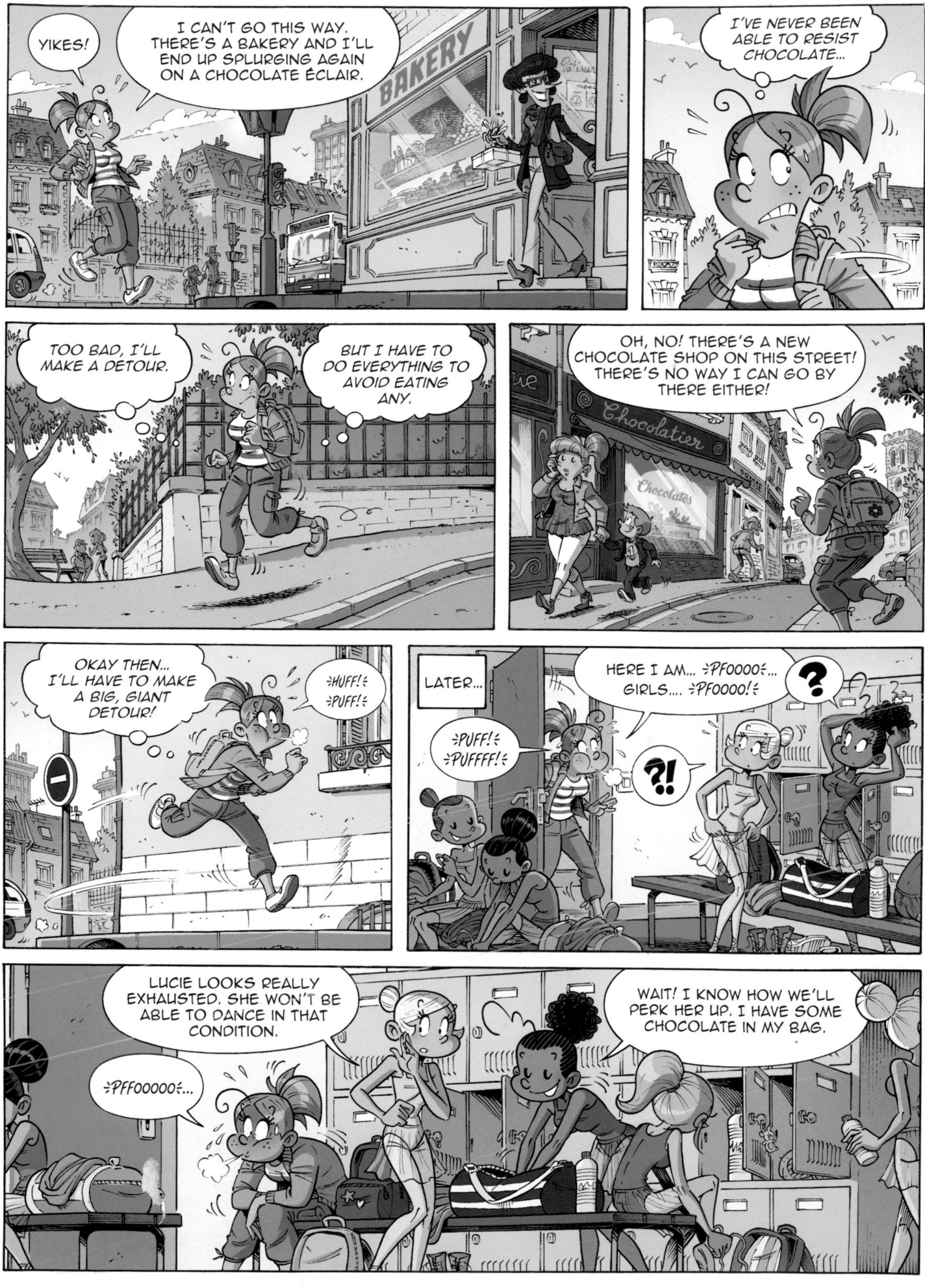
YIKES!
I CAN'T GO THIS WAY. THERE'S A BAKERY AND I'LL END UP SPLURGING AGAIN ON A CHOCOLATE ÉCLAIR.
BAKERY
I'VE NEVER BEEN ABLE TO RESIST CHOCOLATE...
TOO BAD, I'LL MAKE A DETOUR.
BUT I HAVE TO DO EVERYTHING TO AVOID EATING ANY.
OH, NO! THERE'S A NEW CHOCOLATE SHOP ON THIS STREET! THERE'S NO WAY I CAN GO BY THERE EITHER!
Chocolatier
Chocolates
OKAY THEN... I'LL HAVE TO MAKE A BIG, GIANT DETOUR!
HUFF! PUFF!
LATER...
HERE I AM... PFOOOO... GIRLS.... PFOOOO!
?
PUFF! PUFFFF!
?!
LUCIE LOOKS REALLY EXHAUSTED. SHE WON'T BE ABLE TO DANCE IN THAT CONDITION.
WAIT! I KNOW HOW WE'LL PERK HER UP. I HAVE SOME CHOCOLATE IN MY BAG.
PFFOOOOO...

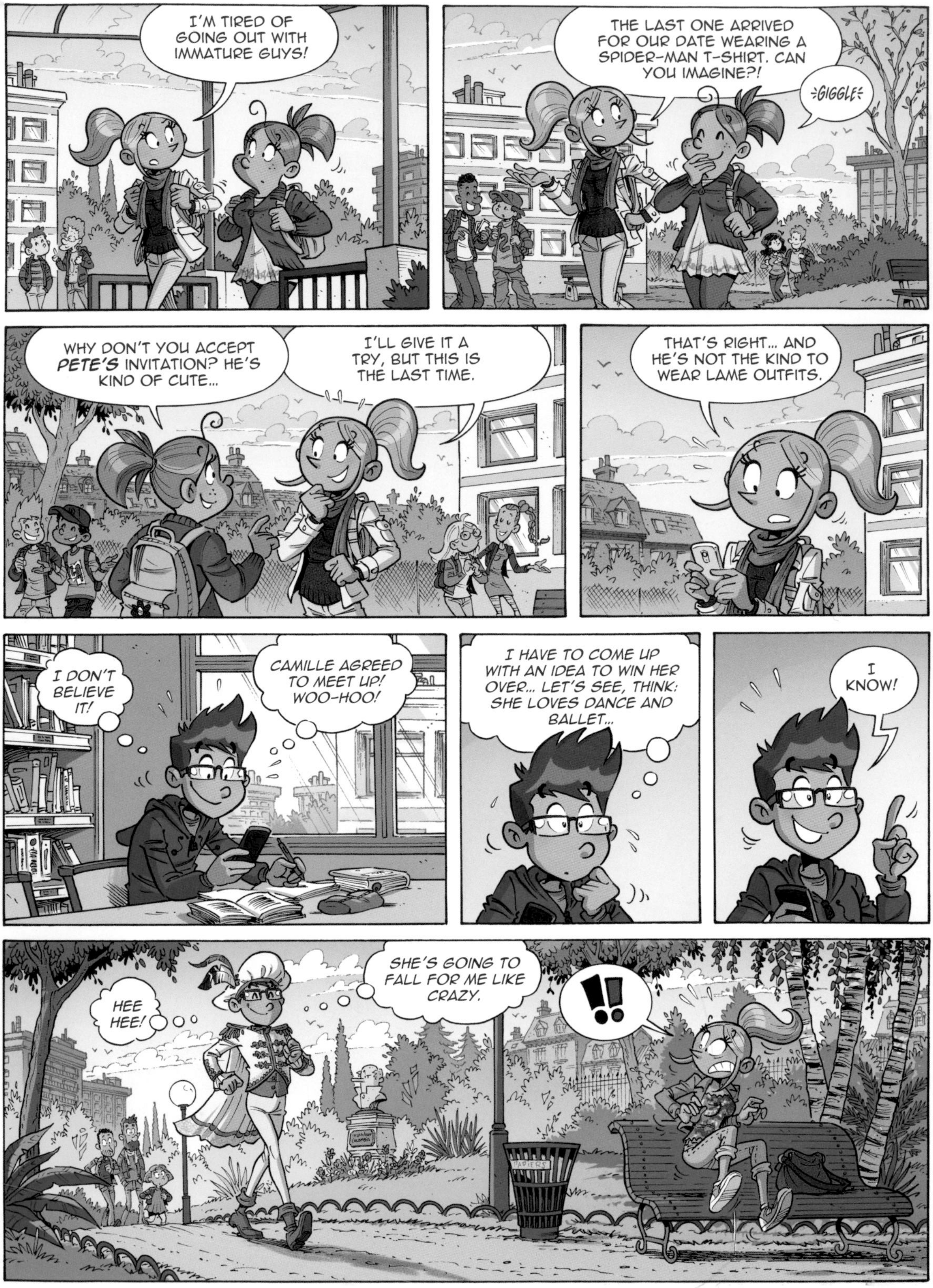

I'M TIRED OF GOING OUT WITH IMMATURE GUYS!
THE LAST ONE ARRIVED FOR OUR DATE WEARING A SPIDER-MAN T-SHIRT. CAN YOU IMAGINE?!
GIGGLE
WHY DON'T YOU ACCEPT PETE'S INVITATION? HE'S KIND OF CUTE...
I'LL GIVE IT A TRY, BUT THIS IS THE LAST TIME.
THAT'S RIGHT... AND HE'S NOT THE KIND TO WEAR LAME OUTFITS.
I DON'T BELIEVE IT!
CAMILLE AGREED TO MEET UP! WOO-HOO!
I HAVE TO COME UP WITH AN IDEA TO WIN HER OVER... LET'S SEE, THINK: SHE LOVES DANCE AND BALLET...
I KNOW!
HEE HEE!
SHE'S GOING TO FALL FOR ME LIKE CRAZY.
!!
PAPIERS

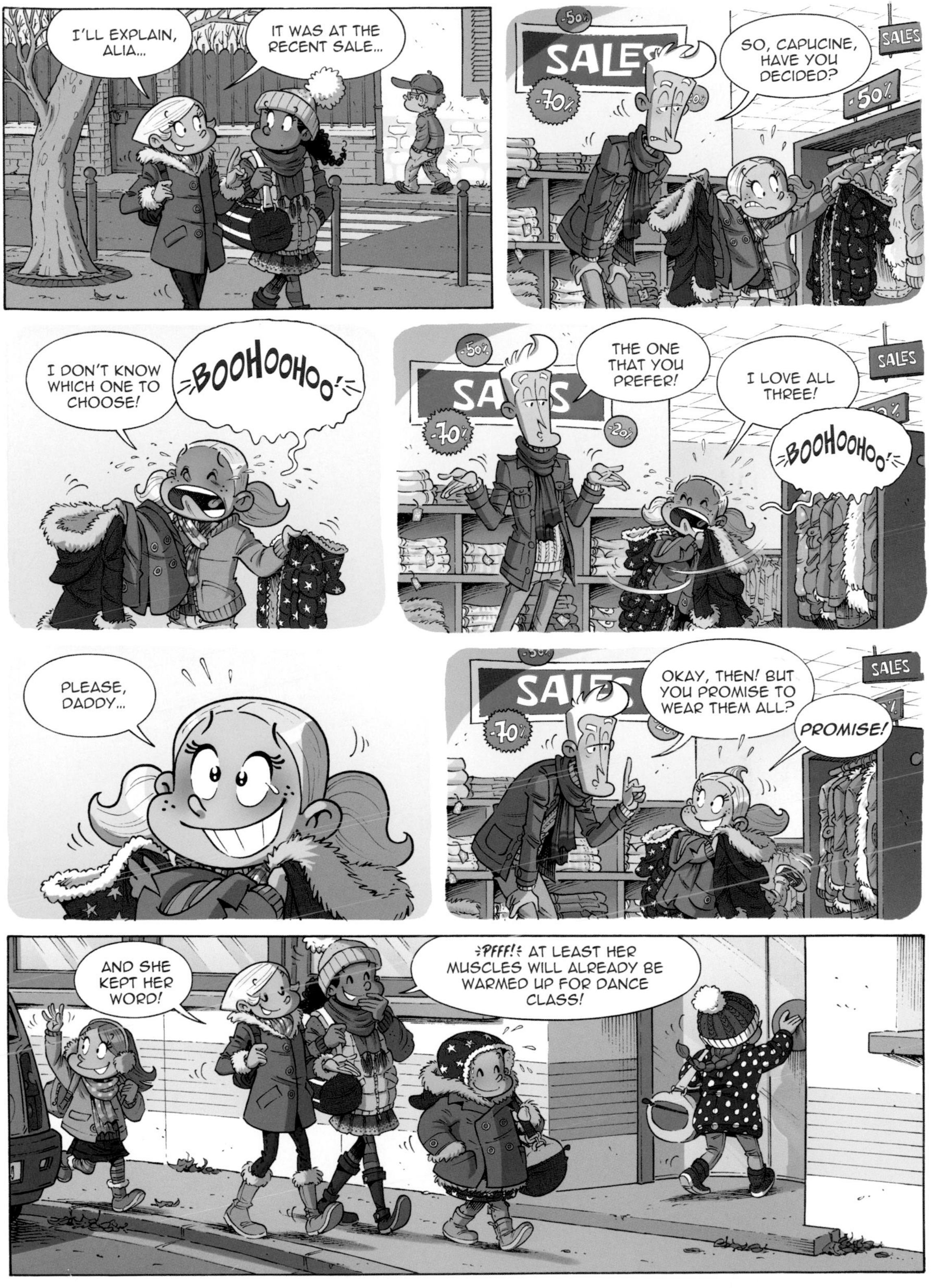
I'LL EXPLAIN, ALIA...
IT WAS AT THE RECENT SALE...
SALES
-50%
-70%
SO, CAPUCINE, HAVE YOU DECIDED?
I DON'T KNOW WHICH ONE TO CHOOSE!
BOOHOOHOO!
THE ONE THAT YOU PREFER!
I LOVE ALL THREE!
BOOHOOHOO!
PLEASE, DADDY...
OKAY, THEN! BUT YOU PROMISE TO WEAR THEM ALL?
PROMISE!
AND SHE KEPT HER WORD!
PFFF! AT LEAST HER MUSCLES WILL ALREADY BE WARMED UP FOR DANCE CLASS!

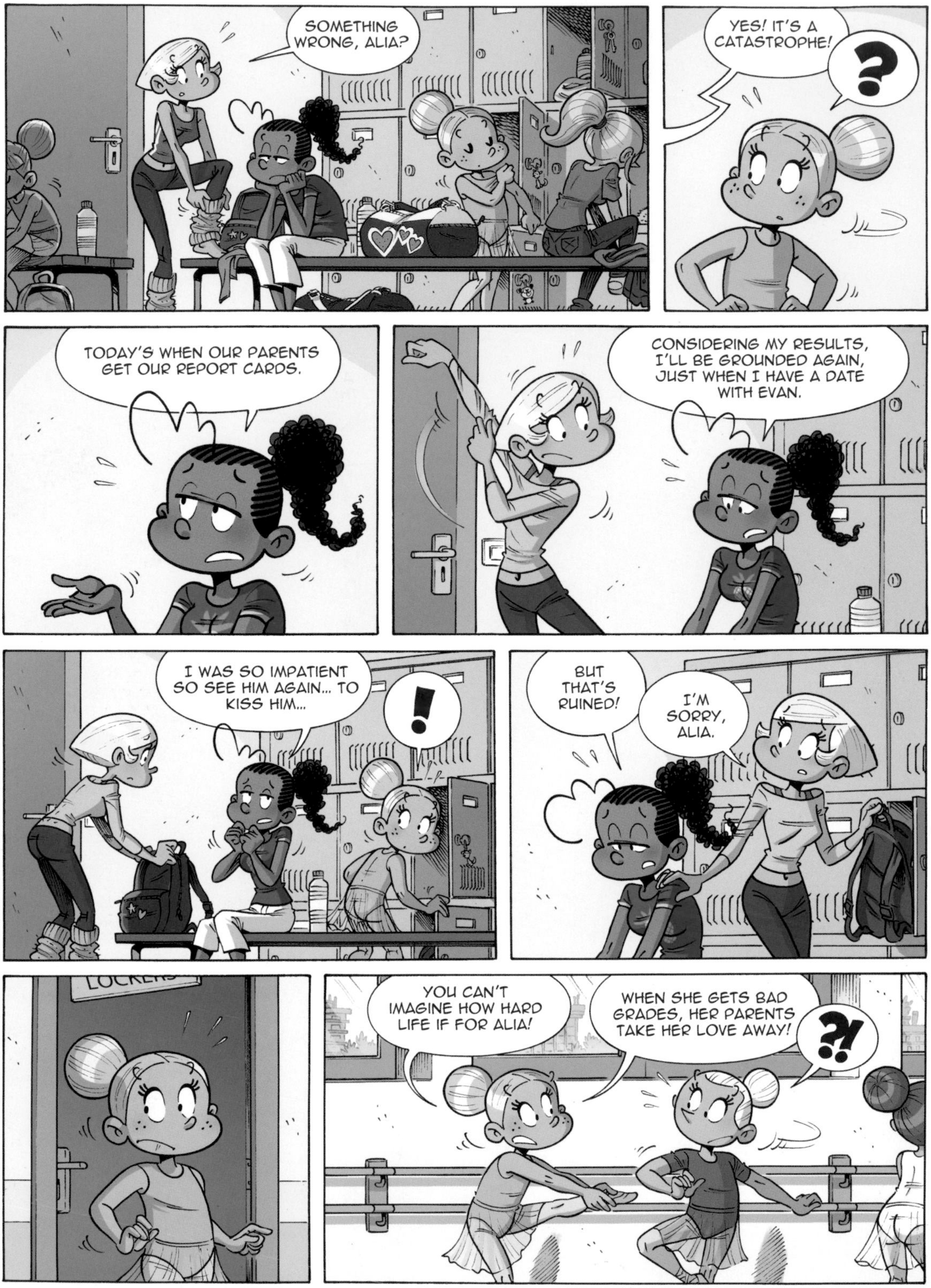
SOMETHING WRONG, ALIA?
YES! IT'S A CATASTROPHE!
?
TODAY'S WHEN OUR PARENTS GET OUR REPORT CARDS.
CONSIDERING MY RESULTS, I'LL BE GROUNDED AGAIN, JUST WHEN I HAVE A DATE WITH EVAN.
I WAS SO IMPATIENT SO SEE HIM AGAIN... TO KISS HIM...
!
BUT THAT'S RUINED!
I'M SORRY, ALIA.
YOU CAN'T IMAGINE HOW HARD LIFE IF FOR ALIA!
WHEN SHE GETS BAD GRADES, HER PARENTS TAKE HER LOVE AWAY!
?!

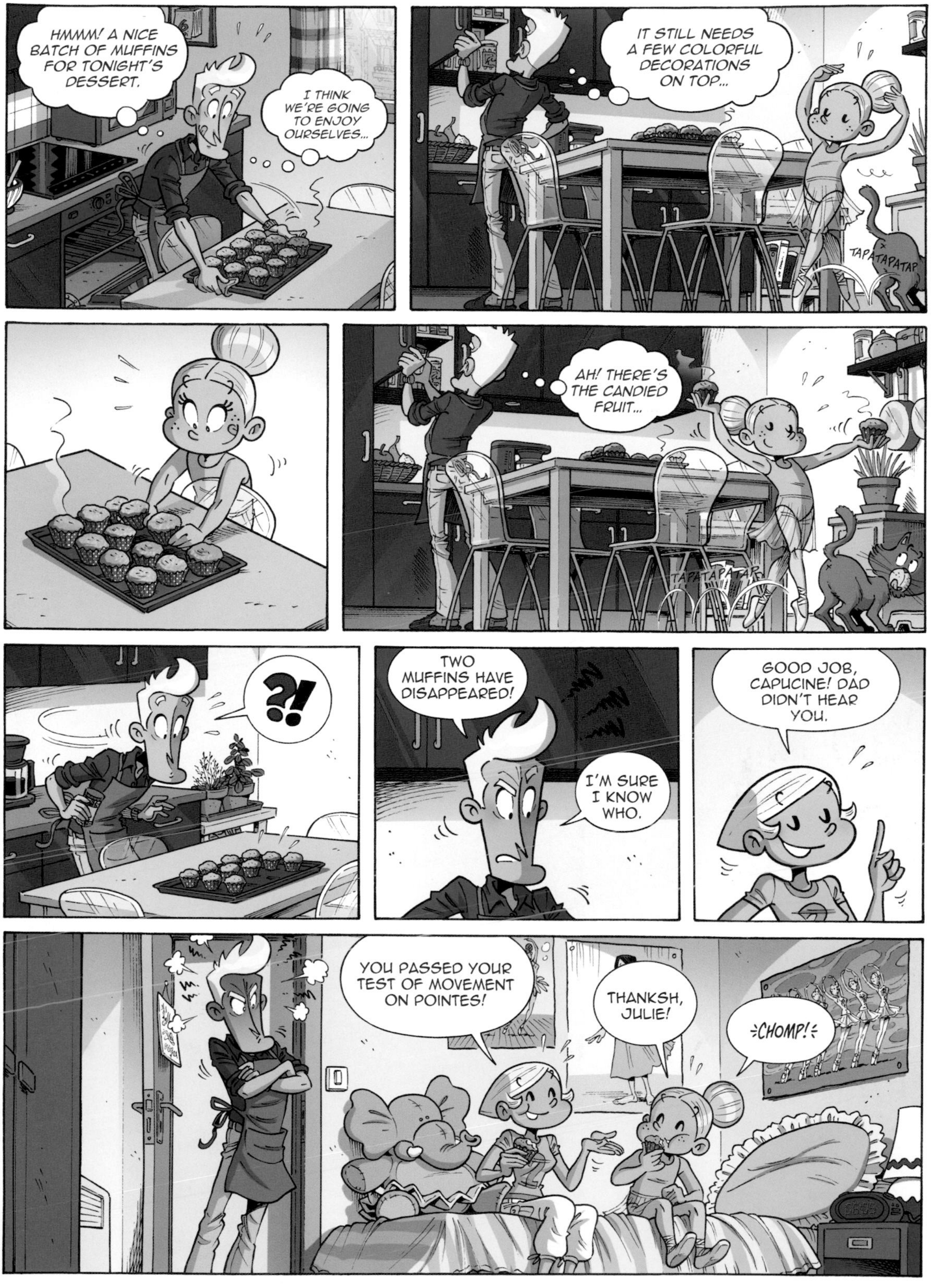
HMMM! A NICE BATCH OF MUFFINS FOR TONIGHT'S DESSERT.
I THINK WE'RE GOING TO ENJOY OURSELVES...
IT STILL NEEDS A FEW COLORFUL DECORATIONS ON TOP...
TAPATAPATAP
AH! THERE'S THE CANDIED FRUIT...
TAPATAPATAP
?!
TWO MUFFINS HAVE DISAPPEARED!
I'M SURE I KNOW WHO.
GOOD JOB, CAPUCINE! DAD DIDN'T HEAR YOU.
YOU PASSED YOUR TEST OF MOVEMENT ON POINTES!
THANKSH, JULIE!
CHOMP!

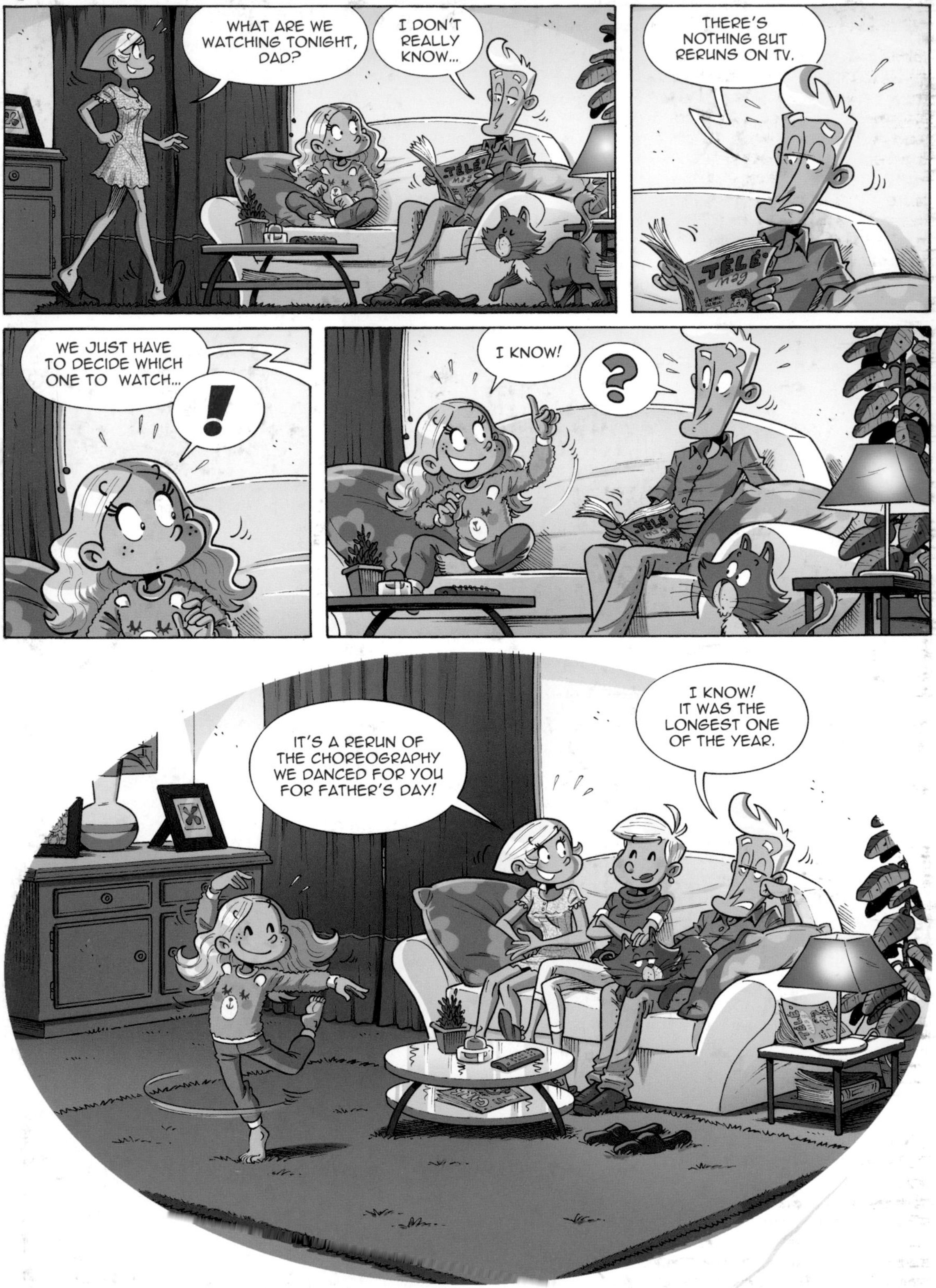

WHAT ARE WE WATCHING TONIGHT, DAD?
I DON'T REALLY KNOW...
THERE'S NOTHING BUT RERUNS ON TV.
WE JUST HAVE TO DECIDE WHICH ONE TO WATCH...
!
I KNOW!
?
IT'S A RERUN OF THE CHOREOGRAPHY WE DANCED FOR YOU FOR FATHER'S DAY!
I KNOW! IT WAS THE LONGEST ONE OF THE YEAR.

WATCH OUT FOR PAPERCUTZ

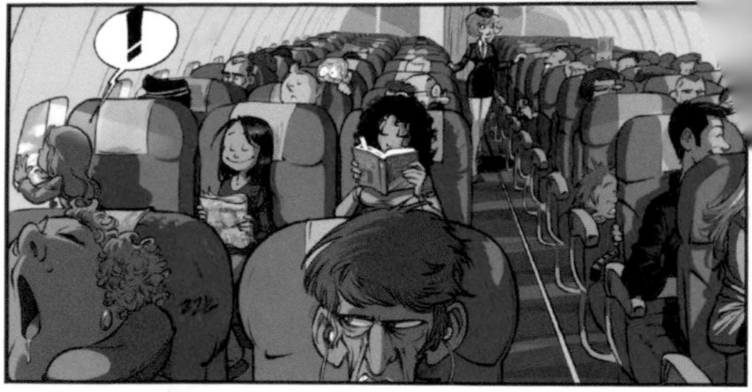
!

¡Hola! Welcome to the enchantingly embracing eleventh DANCE CLASS graphic novel by Crip & Béka, and Maëla Cosson, from Papercutz, those Spanish-language-loving lads and lasses dedicated to publishing great graphic novels for all ages. I'm Jim Salicrup, the part *Español* Editor-in-Chief and global comics fan who enjoys finding out about different people, cultures, and countries from comicbooks. For example, while I'd love to return to Spain right now, that's not really practical during a worldwide pandemic, which is what's happening as I write these words. Instead, I'm able to virtually visit the land of my ancestors through this graphic novel. It's far less expensive—no plane fare or hotel bills—and even far less time-consuming—I can return home in just a second! But Spain isn't the only country you can visit via Papercutz—in DANCE CLASS alone Alia, Julie, and Lucie have visited Paris, France and St. Petersburg, Russia. Here are some of the other places you can visit through the pages of Papercutz…

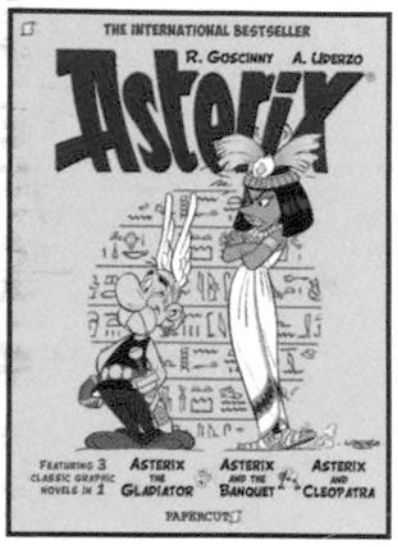
THE INTERNATIONAL BESTSELLER
R. GOSCINNY A. UDERZO
Asterix
FEATURING 3 CLASSIC GRAPHIC NOVELS IN 1
ASTERIX THE GLADIATOR
ASTERIX AND THE BANQUET
ASTERIX AND CLEOPATRA
PAPERCUTZ

Journey back through time to 50 BC in ASTERIX, the international bestselling series by René Goscinny and Albert Uderzo, featuring two gallant Gauls, Asterix and Obelix, fending off the entire Roman Empire from conquering their tiny village. Fortunately, they're aided by a magic potion that makes them invulnerable and super-strong. Which might explain how they're able to visit the Goths in Germania in ASTERIX #1, Cleopatra in Egypt in ASTERIX #2, and Asterix's first cousin once removed in Britain in ASTERIX #3. And they've only just begun, our tireless twosome continue their world tour in future volumes of Asterix, as well.

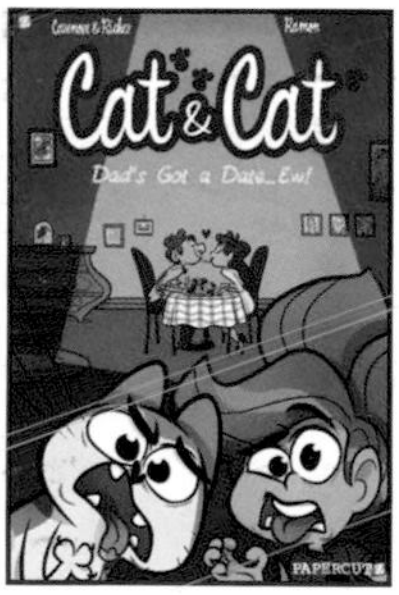
Cat & Cat
Dad's Got a Date...Ew!
PAPERCUTZ

Back to the present, in CAT & CAT #3 "My Dad Has a Date… Ew!" by Cazenove, Richez, and Ramon, Cat's dad, Nathan, takes his new girlfriend, Samantha, and her son, Virgil, along with Cat and her cat, Sushi, on a trip to Venice, Italy, that Sam was hoping to be more romantic and with fewer family members (she especially doesn't appreciate Aunt Philomena!). Can the proposed blended family vacation together and stay together?

Closer to home, Maureen and Wendy, in THE SISTERS #6 "Hurricane Maureen" by Cazenove and William, go across country to visit such famous sites as the Grand Canyon, the Rockies, and Mt. Rushmore. (There are even unofficial cameo appearances of some of the greatest world-travelers in graphic novel history seated in the row behind Maureen, Wendy, and their mom, on the flight home. See top of next column.)

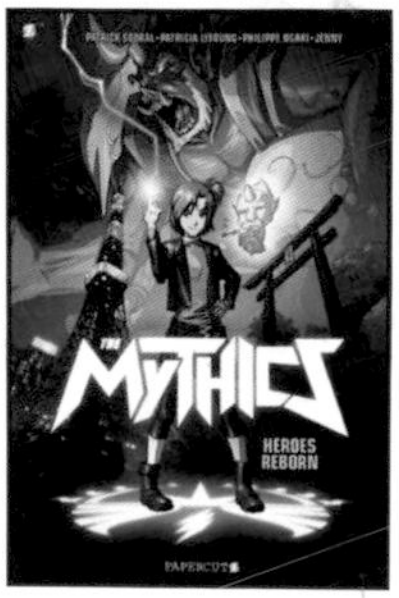
THE MYTHICS
HEROES REBORN
PAPERCUTZ

But perhaps the Papercutz series with the most contemporary globetrotting is THE MYTHICS by Sobral, Lyfoung, Ogaki, and others. This series introduces us to the teenage descendants of the ancient gods who are being summoned to become heroes, with super-powers, to battle an ancient evil. In THE MYTHICS #1 "Heroes Reborn," you'll meet Yuko, a schoolgirl in a rock band, in Japan; Amir, a recently orphaned boy taking over his father's successful company in Egypt; and Abigail, a young opera hopeful in Germany. In THE MYTHICS #2 "Teenage Gods," you'll meet Parvati, an exceptional young student, active in sports, a hospital volunteer, and she even fights crime in her spare time, in India; Miguel, who helps his family by working for a shady businessman, in Mexico; and Neo, who has taken to illegal boxing in fight clubs, in Greece. The writers and artists on THE MYTHICS have not only done an incredible job creating great new heroes but you really do get a feel for what life is like in each character's native land.

We could go on and on, but we think you get the idea! We didn't even mention Geronmo Stilton, who in the GERONIMO STILTON graphic novels, is constantly saving the future, by protecting the past, and traveling all over the world to do so, albeit a somewhat mousier version of our world. Instead, we'll just ask you to keep an eye out for the next DANCE CLASS graphic novel, and to think of Papercutz as your Passport to adventure—even in a pandemic!

Gracias,

Jim

STAY IN TOUCH!

EMAIL: salicrup@papercutz.com
WEB: www.papercutz.com
INSTAGRAM: @papercutzgn
TWITTER: @papercutzgn
FACEBOOK: PAPERCUTZGRAPHICNOVELS
FANMAIL: Papercutz, 160 Broadway, Suite 700, East Wing, New York, NY 10038

MORE GREAT GRAPHIC NOVEL SERIES AVAILABLE FROM

PAPERCUTZ™

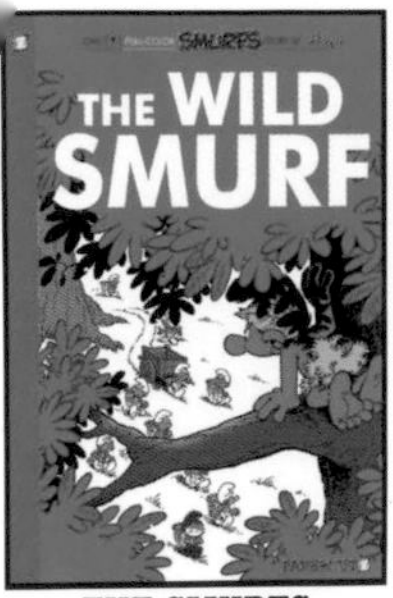
THE WILD SMURF
THE SMURFS

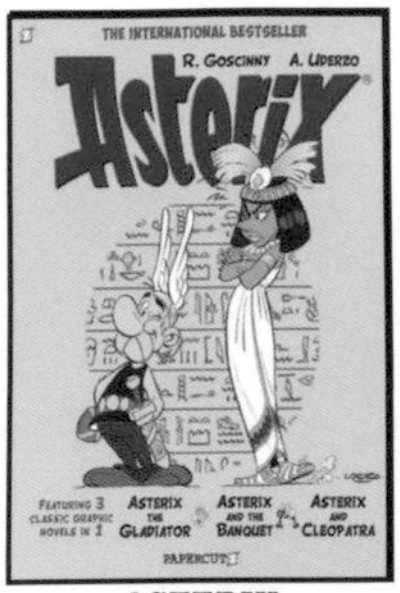
THE INTERNATIONAL BESTSELLER
R. GOSCINNY A. UDERZO
Asterix
Asterix the Gladiator
Asterix and the Banquet
Asterix and Cleopatra
ASTERIX

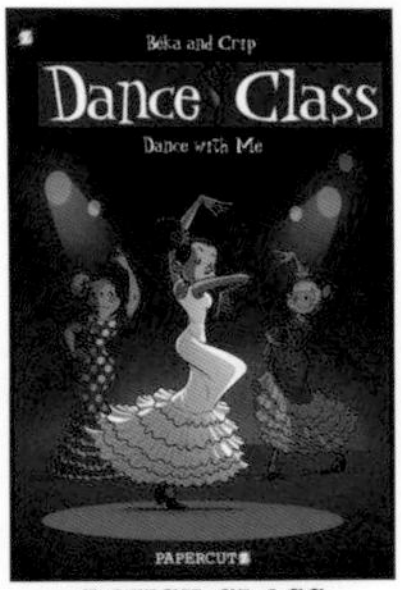
Dance Class
Dance with Me
DANCE CLASS

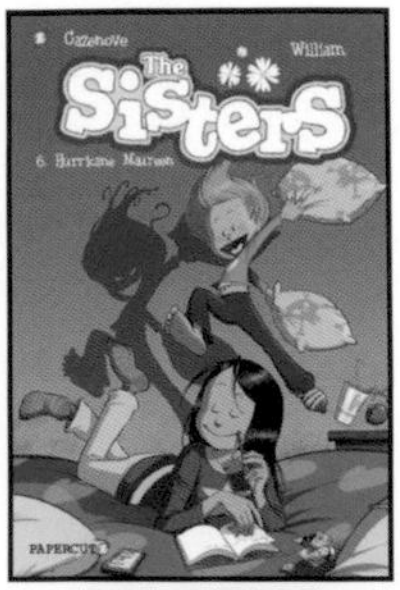
The Sisters
THE SISTERS

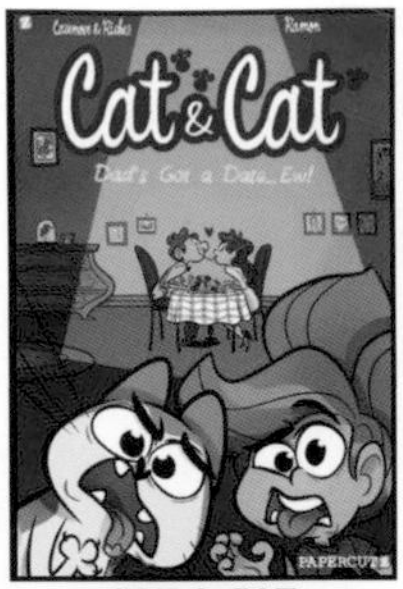
Cat & Cat
CAT & CAT

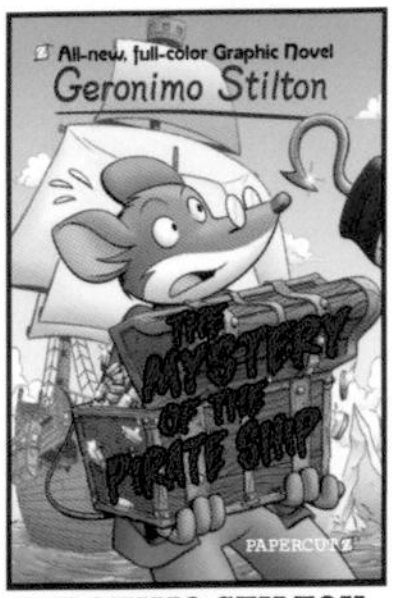
All-new, full-color Graphic Novel
Geronimo Stilton
The Mystery of the Pirate Ship
GERONIMO STILTON

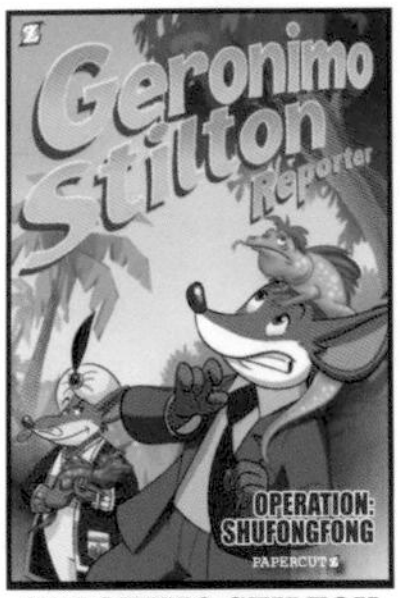
Geronimo Stilton Reporter
OPERATION: SHUFONGFONG
GERONIMO STILTON REPORTER

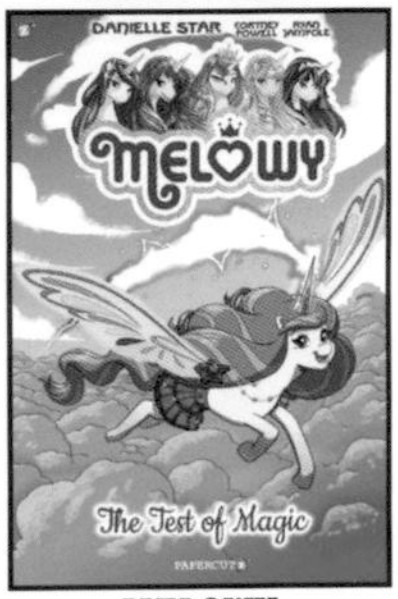
DANIELLE STAR
MELOWY
The Test of Magic
MELOWY

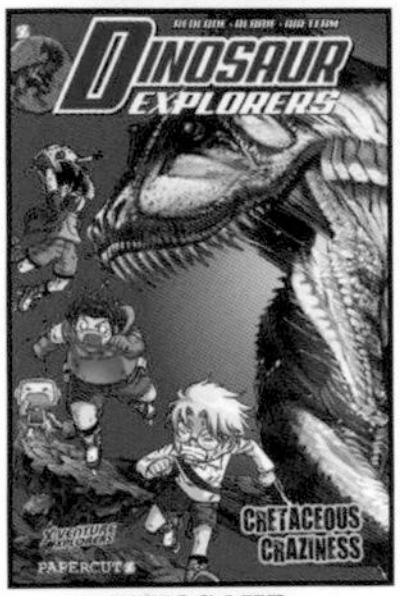
DINOSAUR EXPLORERS
CRETACEOUS CRAZINESS
DINOSAUR EXPLORERS

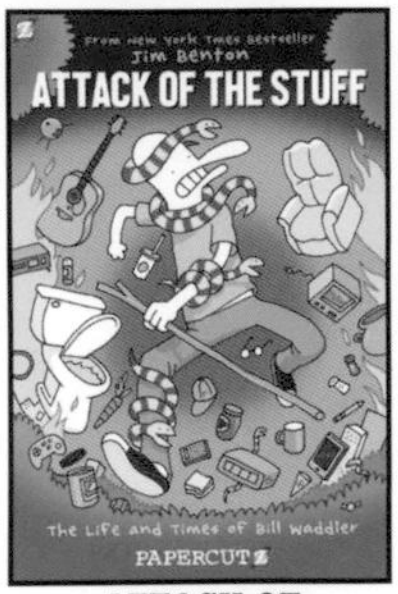
Jim Benton
ATTACK OF THE STUFF
The Life and Times of Bill Waddler
ATTACK OF THE STUFF

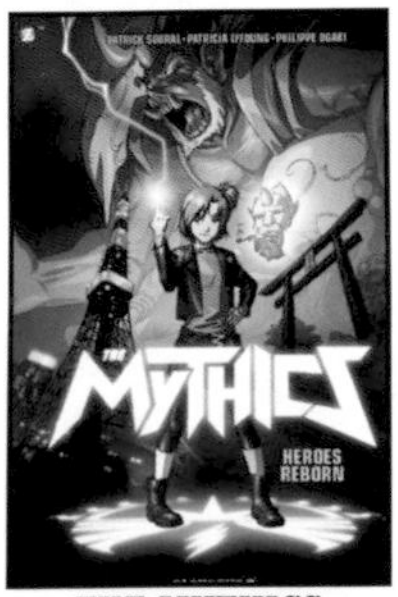
THE MYTHICS
HEROES REBORN
THE MYTHICS

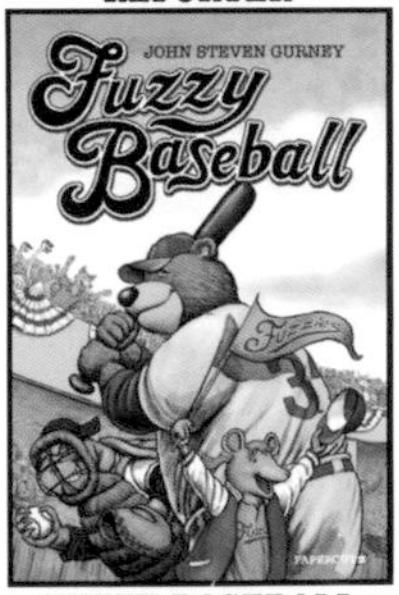
JOHN STEVEN GURNEY
Fuzzy Baseball
FUZZY BASEBALL

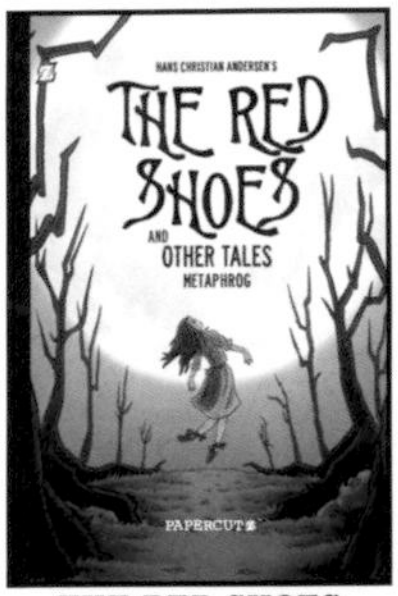
HANS CHRISTIAN ANDERSEN'S
THE RED SHOES
AND OTHER TALES
METAPHROG
THE RED SHOES

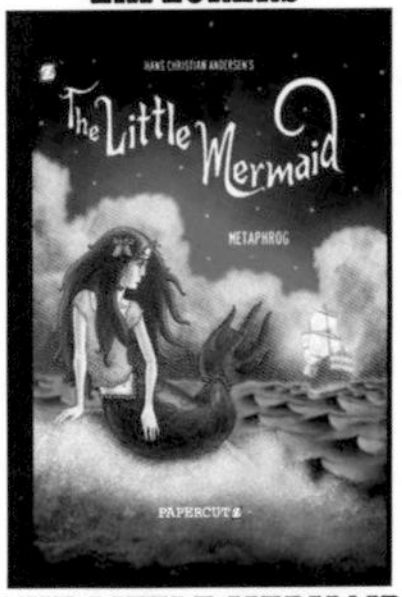
HANS CHRISTIAN ANDERSEN'S
The Little Mermaid
METAPHROG
THE LITTLE MERMAID

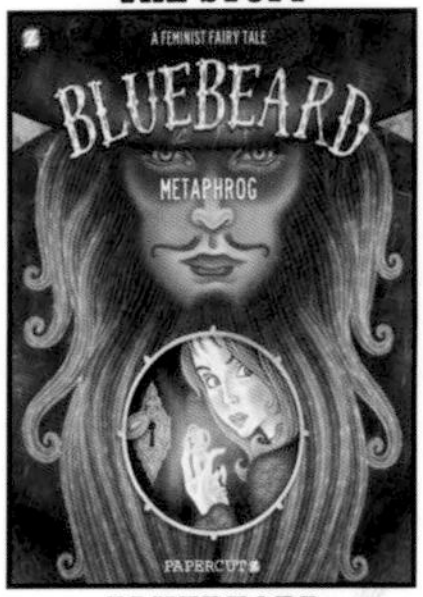
A FEMINIST FAIRY TALE
BLUEBEARD
METAPHROG
BLUEBEARD

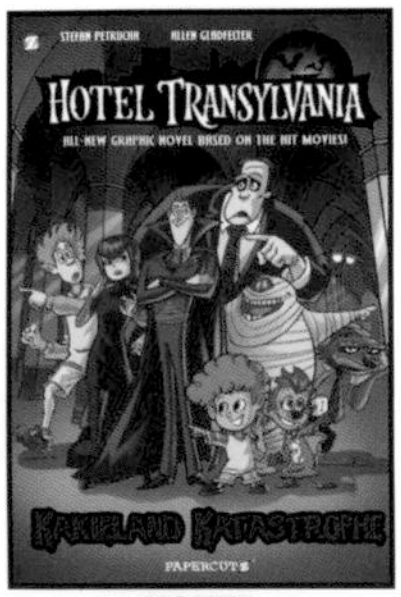
HOTEL TRANSYLVANIA
ALL-NEW GRAPHIC NOVEL BASED ON THE HIT MOVIES!
HOTEL TRANSYLVANIA

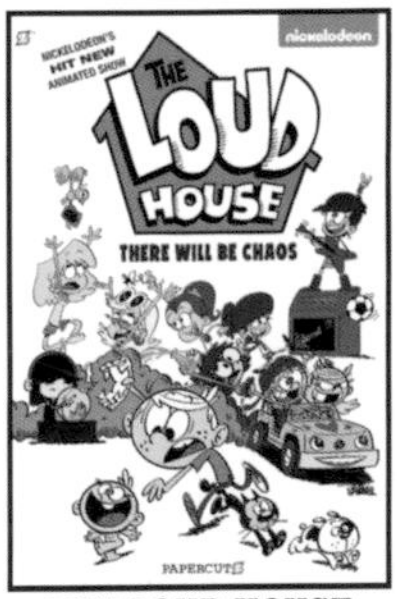
nickelodeon
NICKELODEON'S HIT NEW ANIMATED SHOW
THE LOUD HOUSE
THERE WILL BE CHAOS
THE LOUD HOUSE

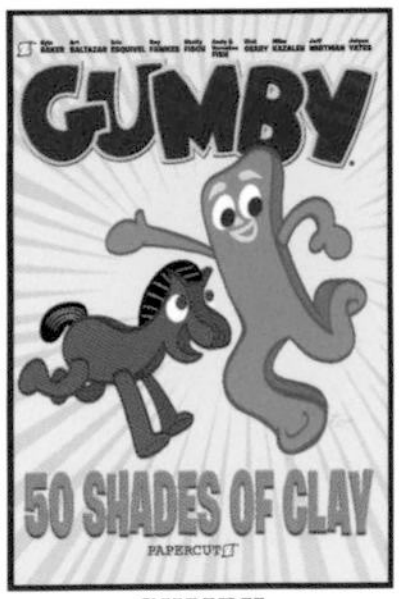
GUMBY
50 SHADES OF CLAY
GUMBY

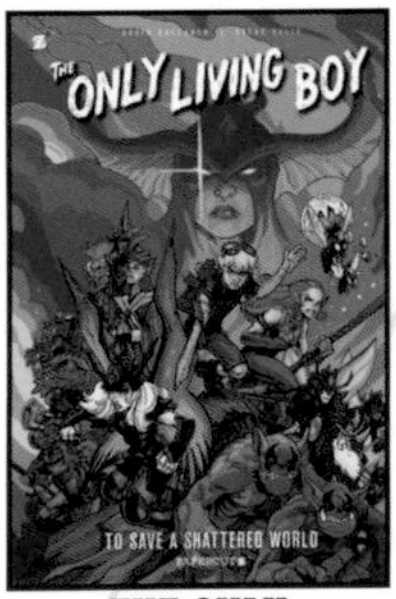
THE ONLY LIVING BOY
TO SAVE A SHATTERED WORLD
THE ONLY LIVING BOY

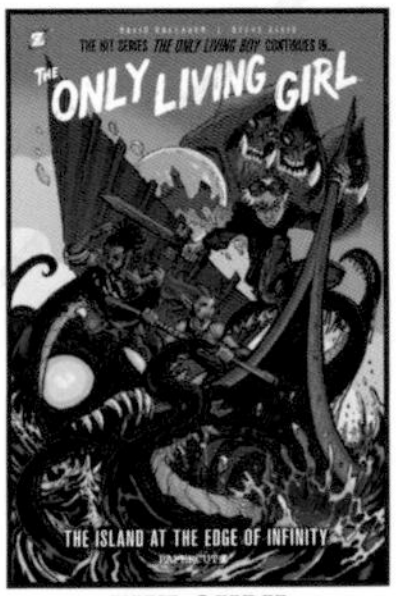
THE ONLY LIVING GIRL
THE ISLAND AT THE EDGE OF INFINITY
THE ONLY LIVING GIRL

Go to papercutz.com for more information

Also available where ebooks are sold.

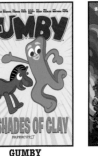

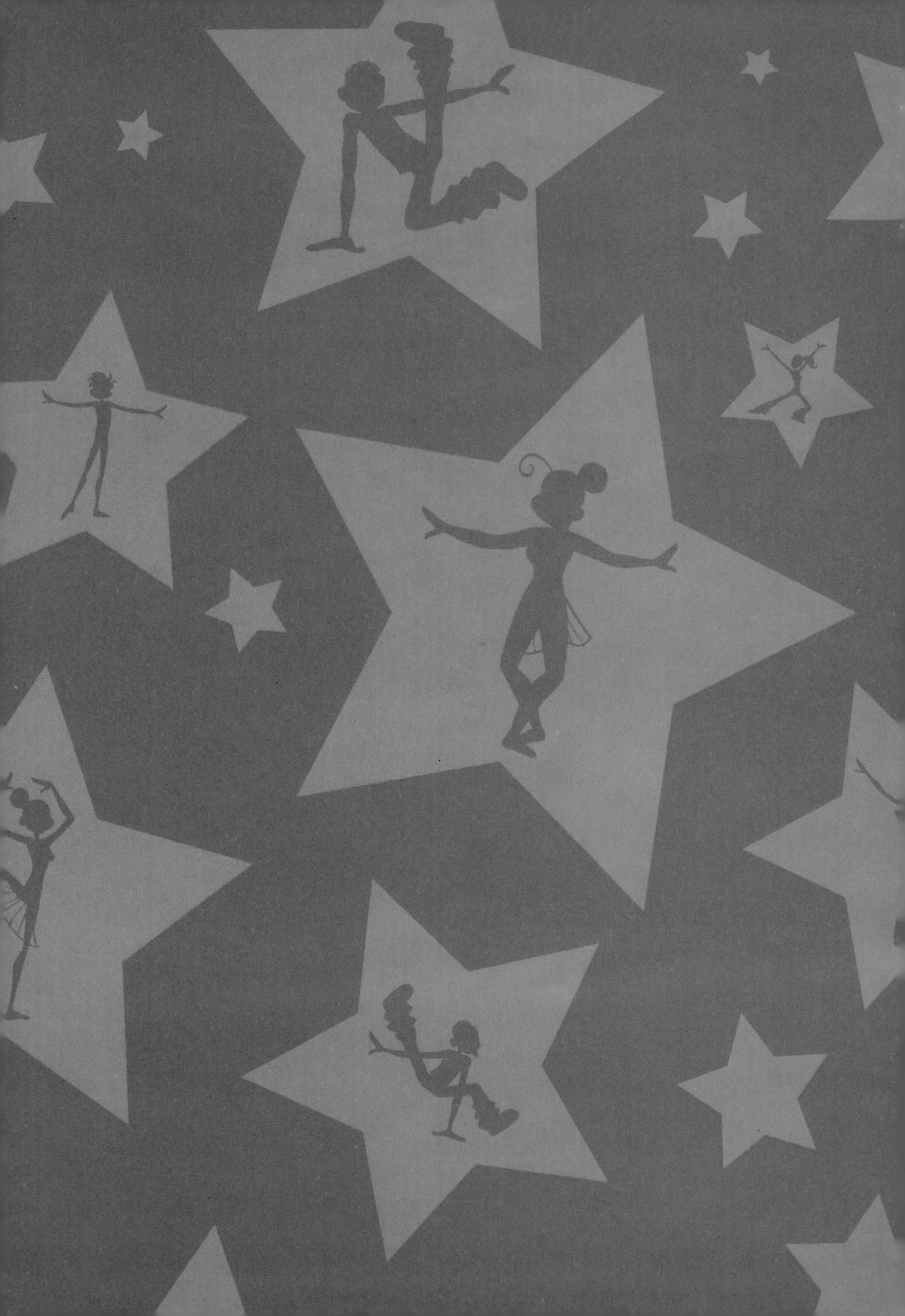